"MASTERS NEXT TO GOD"

"MASTERS NEXT TO GOD"

by
BERNARD EDWARDS

GOMER

First Impression - September 1986

ISBN 0 86383 242 3

Printed by
J. D. Lewis & Sons Ltd., Llandysul, Dyfed

And I have loved thee, Ocean! and my joy
Of youthful sports was on thy breast to be
Borne like thy bubbles, onward: from a boy
I wanton'd with thy breakers—they to me
Were a delight; and if the freshening sea
Made them a terror—'t was a pleasing fear,
For I was as it were a child of thee,
And trusted to thy billows far and near,
And laid my hand upon thy mane—as I do here.

LORD BYRON, The Ocean

for Hildegard—who endured the birth pangs

ACKNOWLEDGEMENT

Captain Daniel and the Pirates, Christmas Rogue and *Sailor's Return* were first published in ''The Seafarer''.

Once Around the World and *A Woman's Place* were broadcast, in shortened form, by BBC Radio Wales in their ''Morning Story'' programme.

AUTHOR'S NOTE

The origin of the phrase ''Master Next to God'' lies deep in the past. To whoever coined it, I give full marks for perception. The master of a merchant ship is truly a man who carries the penultimate in responsibility.

The primary function of the shipmaster is, of course, that of an expert navigator and seaman. He is employed by his Owners to take a ship and her cargo safely and expeditiously from port to port. He might thus be regarded as little more than the long-distance lorry driver of the sea. Many of the uninformed do indeed draw this analogy. But there is more to it than that. During the course of his voyaging, the Master is also solely responsible for the safety, welfare and health of his crew. Again, the critics have been known to say he is no more than the sea-going counterpart of a factory manager ashore. Not such an outstandingly difficult or demanding job —with the added compensation of deckchairs in the sun and duty free gin and tonics before dinner. But what manager ashore has to assume, on a 24 hour basis, the additional roles of doctor, judge and father confessor? What manager has to fight a fire without the services of a fire brigade, handle a riot without the help of the police, bury his own dead and turn his hand to midwifery, when the need arises? All this with his liability under law unlimited and his hours of duty often so unsocial as to make a normal five day week look like a succession of bank holidays.

Yet, despite the pressures, the responsibilities, the criticisms, the shipmaster is one of the few professionals who has never indulged in the popular contemporary game of industrial action. He has often been known to take to the bottle, embrace religion—or both—but his loyalty remains to his ship, his crew and his Owners, in that order.

These stories are purely fictitious, although I cannot deny some of them may have been influenced by people and incidents encountered during my seagoing career. As to the predominantly Welsh flavour, I must crave the indulgence of my foreign readers. I was born in Wales, my permanent anchorage is here. I confess to being unashamedly in love with the place.

Llanvaches   Bernard Edwards
6th September 1984

CONTENTS

CAPTAIN DANIEL AND THE PIRATES   1

ONCE AROUND THE WORLD   9

THE PASSING OF BLACK BEN   19

A WOMAN'S PLACE   42

THE LIGHT THAT KILLED   50

CHRISTMAS ROGUE   59

THE RETURN OF THE FRENCH   69

THE OWNER'S CHOICE   83

FLAGGED OUT   90

IN THE WAKE OF MATTIE JENKINS   99

ACCOUNT SETTLED   109

SAILOR'S RETURN   124

THE FINAL ROUND   132

CAPTAIN DANIEL AND THE PIRATES

The motor vessel *Sultan Ibrahim Omari* sliced her way resolutely through the cobalt blue of the South China Sea, her sleek, clipper bows aimed at the Singapore Strait, gateway to the Indian Ocean and points west. She was also, in my opinion, aiming for serious trouble.

Fifteen thousand tons gross and 575 feet long, the *Omari* was one of a fleet of modern cargo ships employed to carry the wonders of the technological age into the affluent but industrially barren Arabian Gulf. The very latest in coloured televisions, video recorders, cameras and flock upon flock of shiny Toyotas regularly made their one-way journey in her holds. Her owners were a group of Arab merchants predictably hedging their bets against the inevitable passing of the oil wealth. They had named the *Omari* for a recently resurrected ancestor who, it was modestly claimed, had not only been first to circumnavigate the globe but had also invented the steam-reciprocating engine. The ship herself, however, was a far cry from the fantasy world inhabited by her owners. She was the best that petrodollars could buy, having push-button hatches, electric cranes, fully computerised engine-room and enough electronics in the wheelhouse to baffle an astronaut. It was in this wheelhouse that I now stood to attention suffering a strident and typically Welsh harangue delivered by the Master, Captain Daniel Thomas.

'No slant-eyed Chinaman is going to delay my ship, Mister!' he roared, using to the full the considerable power of his large Cardiganshire lungs. 'Not one minute will I delay! We go through the Singapore Strait tonight—and that's final! It is stuff and nonsense to be frightened by talk of pirates.' He glowered down at me. 'What sort of a chief officer are you, eh? No backbone, you English, that's the trouble,' he added in an undertone.

I stood my ground, the sweat soaking into my thin, tropical uniform. The cause of the sweat was not so much

1

fear as auto-suggestion. Although the thermometer in the wheelhouse registered in excess of 100 degrees Fahrenheit, the huge, bearded captain was attired, as always, in a blue, serge suite, high wing collar and shiny, black bowler. Captain Daniel Thomas was an anachronism—a reincarnation of the typical tramp ship master of the early nineteen hundreds, and he revelled in it. He flatly refused to calculate money in anything other than pounds, shillings and pence, regarded ship's engineers as animals to be kept below decks and abhorred all manner of electronic navigational aids. These last, he looked upon as crutches for the incompetent. 'If the electric goes, where are you?' he was fond of pointing out to his junior officers. 'The Good Lord gave you eyes to see, so use them—not that thing!' he would add, aiming a disdainful finger at the sophisticated radar.

I tried the reasonable approach. 'You must be aware, sir, that owing to the danger of attack by pirates, the Owners have advised that we pass through the Singapore Strait in full daylight. It would mean slowing down for only a few hours so that we arrive at the entrance to the Strait at daybreak, rather than in the middle of the night.'

Captain Daniel, who had been pacing the wheelhouse, head down and hands clasped behind his back, offered no comment.

Encouraged, I went on. 'There have been more than thirty attacks on ships in the past month, sir. All at night. We would be tempting Providence . . .'

The Captain came to an abrupt halt in front of me and glowered. 'Tempting Providence, Mister? Are you afraid of a boatload of Chinese coolies, waving rusty, old swords?'

'They are reported to be carrying guns, sir.'

The heavy cane he affected as part of his quaint dress came up and pointed menacingly at my stomach. 'Guns or no guns, I will not slow down my ship, Mister. We go through the Strait tonight and no argument!' He prodded my midriff none too gently. 'Don't worry, young man. Anyone foolish enough to interfere with Captain Daniel Thomas will feel the weight of his 'Pulverisor',' he said, flourishing his cane.

Which was all very well. Captain Daniel's 'Pulverisor', a cane of solid ebony, with its finely carved handle and heavy brass ferrule, was indeed a formidable weapon. It was well known for creating havoc amongst the godowns of Hong Kong and Taiwan, leaving rats, coolies and the odd Customs official prostrate in its wake. But the pirates of the Singapore Strait, manning high-speed launches and carrying automatic rifles, were something else.

'I'll arrange for some extra men on deck,' I said without enthusiasm. It was useless to argue further.

Captain Daniel released the top button of his jacket, his ritual and only concession to the noon-day heat. 'Do that if it will make you feel any safer, young man,' he said disdainfully and, settling his bowler firmly, he marched out of the wheelhouse.

The *Sultan Ibrahim Omari* cruised on at full speed, passing the winking Horsburgh Lighthouse, marking the eastern entrance to the Singapore Strait, at 0300, the darkest hour of the night. Ahead lay three difficult hours weaving through the maze of tiny islands and shoals dotting the narrow strait. On deck, in spite of Captain Daniel's assurances, I was making preparations to ward off the attack I feared. A brace of grenade launchers would have been a help but, in the absence of such deterrents. I was down to basic merchant ship defence strategy. Portable floodlights hung overside illuminating the rushing, black water and, at intervals along the bulwarks, I had stationed my stalwart Pakistani seamen armed with high pressure fire hoses. To my mind, our only hope lay in stopping the pirates at the bulwarks. Once they were on deck, we were done for.

Clutching my personal armament, a thirty-six inch fireaxe handle, I climbed to the bridge to make my report. In the dimly lit wheelhouse, the atmosphere was tense. The helmsman gave a frightened squeal and recoiled to one side when, out of sheer habit, I peered over his shoulder at the compass card. The 2nd Officer, in charge of the watch, was prowling from side to side with all the nervous zeal of a first trip cadet. Catching him in mid-flight, I grabbed his arm. 'Where's the Old Man?' I asked.

If I had put a knife in his back he couldn't have shown more surprise. 'Bloody hell!' he shrieked. Then, recognising me, he let out a sigh of relief. 'Don't ever do that again,' he gasped. 'I thought they were on board already.' He gestured to starboard. 'He's out there.'

The air of nervous apprehension pervading the wheel-house ended abruptly at the starboard door. In the bridge wing, scenting the balmy air and admiring the lights of distant Singapore, Captain Daniel was slowly perambulating, at peace with the world. 'A fine night, Mister,' he observed on sighting me. 'Cardigan Bay weather, this.'

'Yes, sir,' I agreed without comment. On my one and only passage of Cardigan Bay it had been raining stair rods and blowing force ten.

'What's that you have got, then?' the Captain asked, indicating my fireaxe handle.

I hefted the weapon. 'We're standing by to repel boarders, sir,' I said and went on to explain the precautions in hand.

When I had finished, he sniffed. 'A waste of time, boy. But carry on if it pleases you.'

I left the bridge wondering if I was taking a far too serious view of the situation.

★   ★   ★   ★

The attack came shortly after five o'clock, as the first streaks of dawn were painting the sky astern and my sleep-starved mind was crowded with jumbled images of eggs, sunny-side-up, crisp rashers of bacon and soft, feminine curves waiting in a double bed in far away Norfolk. Taking advantage of the half-light, a dark shape crept up on the star-board quarter and, with a sharp ring of steel on steel, grapp-ling irons flew over the bulwarks. A sing-song Asian voice cried, 'Lookout! Bloody pirates coming!' and the seamen on guard in the threatened area formed a loose scrum as they fought to vacate the deck. Using my fireaxe handle to good effect, I forced the stampeding men back to their posts and, at my signal, hydrants were wrenched open and four powerful jets caught the pirate launch in a wicked cross-fire of high-pressure water. Crouching low at the bulwark, I waited for a fusilade of shots in return but heard only screams of rage and anguish. The boarding ropes suddenly went slack and I raised my head to see the launch sheering off to be left rolling help-lessly in the wake thrown up by the *Omari's* thrusting prop-ellor. Relief flooded over me. I had soundly trounced the so-called pirates of the Singapore Strait.

Bursting with pride, I turned to make my way up to the bridge and came face to face with a sextet of the meanest looking, slant-eyed brown-skinned characters it has ever been my misfortune to encounter. Not a man over five feet tall but each of them pointing a lethal-looking Armalite in my general direction. There was no doubt but that I had been neatly and thoroughly outmanoeuvered. The launch on the starboard quarter had obviously been a decoy, holding my attention while this bunch of brigands boarded unopposed on the port side of the ship.

Surprised, horrified and scared as I was, my mind was still able to take in the fact that the men were identically dressed in knee-length loincloths, with brightly coloured headbands binding their long, black hair. Possibly Chinese but more likely Indonesians, I thought. The central figure, whom I assumed to be the leader, sported a thin, straggling mous-tache of the kind popular with a previous generation of Orientals. He now moved quickly forward and rammed his gun barrel into my churning stomach. 'Hands up, English-man!' he spat, wafting the stench of stale garlic in my face. 'We go to blidge, quick! No funny business or you dead, okay?'

Now, had I been an Englishman of the old Raj, I would no doubt have set about this stinking little man. I was, how-ever, no more than an ineffectual British merchant seaman of the 1980's caught with his pants down around his ankles. Moreover, a sharp prod in the region of my left kidney warned me that I was surrounded. Not wishing to end up minus several essential internal organs, I dropped my club and raised my hands high. 'This way, gentlemen,' I croaked and set off at the head of the villainous band, feeling for all the world like the proverbial condemned man taking his last walk. It had, of course, occurred to me that, if the pirates failed to dispose of me, Captain Daniel most certainly would.

Our orderly procession broke up when we reached the bridge ladder, which was a bare 24 inches wide and designed for the passage of one person at a time. The pirates, evidentally well versed in the art of community life, insisted on climbing the ladder in a tight-knit bunch—with me in the middle. There was a great deal of muttered cursing and elbow-jabbing, during which I lost not only the remains of my dignity but much of my shirt, which was already soaked and filthy from my night's work. When I finally stumbled into the wheelhouse, I must have been a very sorry sight indeed.

Captain Daniel was ensconced in the high pilot chair in front of the wheelhouse windows contemplating the dark horizon ahead. At my sudden and undignified entrance, he turned with a frown. 'I'll have none of that rowdiness up here, if you please, Mister,' he growled. Receiving no reply, he eased his large bulk down from the chair and came closer. Looking down at me from his great height, he took in my dishevelled appearance and tut-tutted. 'Had a bit of an accident have you, young man?' he rumbled with the ghost of a smile.

I indicated the shadows behind me. 'We . . . we've been boarded, sir,' I said weakly, 'Pirates.' At which point, I was pushed roughly aside and the pirate leader stepped forward brandishing his gun at Captain Daniel. 'You Captain?' he asked in a high-pitched, belligerent voice.

Captain Daniel leaned forward, peering shortsightedly. 'What's this?' he said sharply, then proceeded to prod the fierce little man's chest with his 'Pulverisor'. 'Ah . . . John Chinaman—eh! Well . . . there's nothing here for you, my man. Get off my ship this minute! Do you understand?'

I groaned aloud and waited for the bullets to fly.

The pirate leader staggered back, a look of astonishment on his face. He rattled the bolt of his gun angrily. 'Big,

English bastard!' he screamed. 'You my prisoner, now. We go your cabin, open safe. Want all money!' At the mention of the last word, the rest of the gang closed up on the Captain with a chorus of rattling bolts.

Captain Daniel was oblivious to the danger, his face livid. He drew himself up to his full height. 'Bastard I may be, John Chinaman,' he roared. 'But I am Welsh, not English! There is a difference, see.'

The farce had gone far enough. 'Don't be a fool, sir!' I hissed. 'They'll kill you.'

He held up his hand. 'Please attend to the navigation, Mister,' he said calmly. 'I will deal with this scum. A taste of my 'Pulverisor' is what they need.' With that, moving with amazing speed for a man his age and weight, he put his back to the flag locker and swung his cane in an arc, covering the hesitantly advancing pirates.

You stupid, brave old man, I thought. You're not up against a bunch of dockside coolies now. These boys will blow your stubborn, old Welsh head off.

Then, as I screwed up my courage to go to his aid, the brass ferrule of Captain Daniel's 'Pulverisor' ejected and went spinning to the deck. There was a loud bang and a great sheet of orange flame spurted from the muzzle-like aperture in the end of the cane. In one fell swoop, the pirate leader's colourful headband and much of his hair disappeared, the armoured glass of the window behind him shattered into a million pieces and the wheelhouse was filled with choking, black smoke.

Deathly silence followed. Then, out of the blackness, came the unearthly screams. When the smoke cleared, I looked around for the carnage, for the twitching bodies and the oozing blood. Nothing. Only the bare backside of the last of the pirate gang arching through the air as its owner, minus loincloth and God knows what else, followed his brothers over the bulwark rail. I ran out of the wheelhouse and craned over the side to see all six vanquished robbers swimming strongly away from the ship like a pack of escaping rats.

Returning inside, I found Captain Daniel using a pull-through on his 'Pulverisor'. 'Did you know we Welsh invented gunpowder?' he said calmly, without looking up from his task.

I was so shaken by the recent events that there was no argument in me.

'Trouble is,' he went on, 'we never learned how to control the damn thing properly.' He looked up at the shattered window and shook his head sadly. 'Quarter of an ounce too much that time, I think. 'You'd better get a new glass in there, Mister, before the Owners find out.'

ONCE AROUND THE WORLD

It is winter eight months of the year in Pembrokeshire and, in these dismal months, Dinas Coch is no place for those who would live the comfortable life. This steep sided indent in St. Brides Bay is an open wound constantly probed by the keening, rain-laden winds of the North Atlantic. On the rare occasions when the wind, through sheer exhaustion, falls still, the slate-grey waters of the inlet lie quiescent beneath a blanket of dense fog, penetrated only by the warning bleat of the foghorn on Carreg-mawr, two miles offshore.

On such a day, 'Cap'n Once' and his bride, Angharad, set sail from Dinas Coch to circumnavigate the world. Witnessing their departure, a small knot of villagers led by my father, the vicar of St. Agnes, stood on the quayside in the pouring rain and sang several verses of 'For Those in Peril on the Sea', as the 32-foot, blue-painted, ex-Cardigan herring drifter slid disconsolately into the fog banks assembling on the horizon. I was just sixteen at the time and it lay heavy on my young conscience that I was principally responsible for the whole farce.

It had all started the summer before; and summer in Dinas Coch, I can assure you, is sheer beauty. It is that brief season set aside by the relenting gods to repay a thousandfold the flagellations of winter. The warm sun strikes flecks of gold on the tranquil, blue waters of the inlet, campion and cornflower draw a patchwork quilt of pink and blue across the rocky cliff faces and cattle chew contentedly in the lush grass, which rolls back, field upon field, to where the purple-tinted Precelly mountains merge into a cloudless sky. Even now that I am a grown man, summer in Dinas Coch never fails to seduce me.

The first day of my summer holidays that year proved to be no exception to the rule. As I cycled through the early-morning stirrings of Main Street, I savoured the six whole weeks of carefree idleness which lay ahead of me. Crystal clear mornings with the mackerel plopping in the placid waters of the bay, lazy afternoons roaming the gorse-covered hillsides, long, twilit evenings around a driftwood fire, with roast potatoes burnt on the outside, hot and floury inside, and the squeals of girls being chased, and caught, amongst the sand dunes. This was to be my just reward for another dreary year spent at Llangarron College, where dry-as-dust Latin, higher mathematics and liberal helpings of theology stupefied my sensitive, young mind. At the start of that long-to-be-remembered summer there was just one tiny cloud on my horizon. I was flat broke.

Being a son of a clergyman in the Church of Wales, I had been brought up in a world of genteel poverty. My father, devout man though he was, had an unfortunate weakness for the gymnastics of the bedroom, while my mother had never been known to say no to anything—until it was too late. As a result, I was one of eight perpetually hungry, shabbily dressed but well-mannered vicarage children. As the eldest son, I enjoyed the doubtful privilege of being educated at Llangarron College, a prison-like establishment reserved for the sons of impoverished clergymen. Llangarron did, however, have its compensations. The college was a hotbed of illicit financial enterprises. My current involvement was a book of Irish Sweepstake tickets, entrusted to me as sole agent for Dinas Coch by Isaac Lewis, the college grounds-man. 'Ten percent of the takings for you, boyo,' Isaac wheezed as he stuck the book into my back pocket, his hand spending an inordinately long time on my bum in the process. Dirty old man was Isaac.

Now there was a considerable potential for profit in this project. Ten percent of twenty-five tickets at a pound apiece was not to be sneezed at, and would certainly cover my holiday spending nicely. Moreover, the prizes were big and there was always the chance that a grateful beneficiary would grease my palm. But complete secrecy was essential. Should my father get wind of my involvement in the Turf, I was in deep trouble. For this reason, I had decided to approach only my close friends in the village. 'Cap'n Once' was at the top of this list.

When I freewheeled down to the quay, the captain was still out inspecting his lobsterpots. I sat warming myself in the sun for a good half an hour before he came put-putting through the early morning haze hanging over the harbour entrance.

'Catch, Davy!' he called, throwing me a rope as he awkwardly manouvered his converted ship's lifeboat alongside the quay wall. The noise of wood splintering on stone was enough to set your teeth on edge.

He scrambled nimbly up onto the quay and pumped my hand enthusiastically. 'So good to see you again, Davy,' he bubbled. You would think I had been to the moon, instead of up the line to Llangarron.

Owain Evans, to give him his real name, was a small, wiry man—nearer sixty than fifty—with curly black hair greying at the temples and a ruddy, wind-seared complexion. Laughter was never far from his lips but, sometimes, a veil of sadness would pass fleetingly across his eyes. In a village built on generations of sea-captains, 'Cap'n Once' was not a name to bear lightly.

'Cap'n Once' was a master mariner all right—passed by the Board of Trade in Cardiff and proud of it. But his first and only command had been a comedy of errors. Sailing from Newport, Mon. with a cargo of coal for the Far East, he had inaugurated his new command by ramming and sinking the lock gates as he left the port. This misfortune was quickly followed by a collision with the pilot cutter off Barry Roads. Several irate pilots, a cat and a foul-mouthed parrot were left struggling in the murky waters of the Bristol Channel without a lifejacket or a tot of whisky between them.

The final blow had also fallen on that eventful night. Captain Evans, seeking to comfort a distraught lady missionary —passenger in the ship to Sumatra—had plied her, and himself, with his best madeira. As often happens when emotion and alcohol meet, the captain and the good lady soon found themselves enjoying the delights of two-in-a-bed. Unfortunately, the direction of the ship was left entirely in the hands of the 1st Mate, a notorious tippler from Abersoch, who conned the ship down Channel through a thickening haze generated by frequent and liberal draughts of Johnny Walker Red Label.

Come morning, the poor, ill-used vessel was high and dry on Ilfracombe Beach and a total loss. Captain Evans, on his inglorious return to Dinas Coch, became 'Cap'n Once' and seemed doomed to carry that derisory title to his grave.

'How's business, Cap'n?' I asked, when he had settled himself alongside me on the warm stone of the quayside. Apart from the lobsters, he made a fair living from running summer visitors out to the wreck on Carreg-mawr.

'Not too good, Davy,' he answered, fishing in the pockets of his old reefer jacket and finally discovering his short-stemmed briar. He blew hard into the pipe, sending a shower of dottle high into the air. He packed the pipe with thick, brown shag and shook his head. 'The lobsters bring good money, you know, Davy. The posh hotels can't get enough of them. But people don't want boat trips any more. All off to Spain for their holidays, see.'

Putting a match to his pipe, he puffed thoughtfully, enveloping himself in a cloud of evil-smelling smoke. After a good cough he went on, 'Not that I blame them, of course. But I can't live on the lobsters alone, Davy. I must leave Dinas Coch.'

A lone seagull wheeled menacingly overhead but did little more than empty its bowels aimlessly into the wind.

'Where will you go?' I asked. 'What will you do?' I couldn't imagine Dinas Coch without 'Cap'n Once'.

He got to his feet and peered out to sea, screwing up his eyes until the wrinkles appeared. When he spoke, his voice was quiet but determined. 'I will sail around the world, Davy.'

Now I knew the old bugger was mad. 'Around the world!' I repeated incredulously. 'In that thing?' pointing down at the aged lifeboat tugging feebly at its moorings.

'No, David *bach*.' There was a new light in his eyes. 'A new boat I will have. Twice the size of that. And I will command her around the world. I will be owner, master and crew. No-one will be able to take her from me.' Then, he shook his head sadly. 'Terrible lot of money it will cost. But it's either that or marry Angharad Morris . . .'

He said it as though he had not spent the past fifteen years shyly courting Angharad Morris—with never a sign from her, other than a basket of fresh-baked scones left outside the door of his cottage every Saturday afternoon, regular as clockwork.

I took my cue and produced the book of sweepstake tickets. Within minutes, I had convinced 'Cap'n Once' that the way to his new boat and the circumnavigation of the world lay through the Irish Sweepstake. Even then, he was cautious, not going beyond a half-share at ten shillings.

'And make sure you sell the other half to Angharad Morris! I can trust her, ' he called after me as I stiff-pedalled up the steep path away from the quay. I smiled knowingly. A plan was beginning to form in the back of my mind.

Young Dolly Pritchard was scrubbing the front steps of the *Dinas Arms*, displaying her knickers to all and sundry, as I coasted past. 'Morning, Dolly! There's a lovely bum you've got!' I called.

She scrambled to her feet, pulling in vain at the hem of her mini-skirt. 'You dirty thing, David Price!' she shouted back. 'And you the vicar's son, too.'

I blew her a cheeky kiss and swerved across the road to where Angharad Morris was polishing the already sparkling windows of the *Pentre Tea Shop*. In her native Rhondda clean windows were next to godliness.

With a squealing of brakes, I drew up and called a breezy, 'Good morning, Mrs. Morris.'

Pausing in her work, Angharard folded her arms over her lovely bosom and examined me with her head on one side. '*Duw*! There's a fine young man you are growing into, Davy,' she said in her soft, melodious voice. 'A cup of tea you want, is it?'

Needing no second invitation, I followed her through the shop door with its familiar tinkling bell. She sat me down at a dark oak table smelling of beeswax and, with the morning sun filtering through the chintz-curtained windows, I ploughed my way through three mugs of scalding tea and a small mountain of crumbling, hot scones spread with yellow, salty butter fresh from the farm. Breakfast at the vicarage had been the usual burnt toast and watery coffee.

She fussed over me like a mother hen, the occasional soft press of her breast on my shoulder as she bent over me and the heady scent of violets—bottled by the monks on Caldy Island—sending funny shivers up and down my spine.

Angharad Morris was a fine looking woman. Pretty, in the dark way of the valley people, her forty two years showed only as flecks of grey in her tumbling, black hair and the beginnings of a matronly spread in her rounded hips. Panted over by half the able-bodied men in the village, she was. I often wished myself twenty years older so that I might pant with the rest.

She had had a terribly sad life although, since she was always ready for a laugh, you would hardly think so. She came from the Rhondda Valley, young and silly, to marry Ossie Morris, fifteen years her senior but as handsome as they come in his brass-bound uniform of the Customs & Excise. Angharad had paid for her mistake with six years of marriage tormented by drink and physical abuse until, one winter's night, Ossie had obliged her by stepping off Pencaer Cliffs into the gale-swept sea below. At the inquest it was established that Officer Morris was not engaged on Her Majesty's business at the time of the accident, nor was he entirely sober. The subsequently reduced widow's pension was a mere pittance. But Angharad, being of Welsh mining stock, was not one to take things lying down. With the help of Edward Lewis-the-Bank—secretly in love with her, of course—the tea shop had been set up and had prospered. The brutality of her marriage Angharad forgave and forgot but never the barrennes of it. For babies she would have endured a dozen of Ossie Morris.

When I had finished every last crumb of my second breakfast, I sat back fit to burst. 'Been waiting for that all term, I have, Mrs. Morris,' I gasped.

'Starve you at that old school do they, my lovely?' she smiled. 'Shame on them!'

While she busied herself clearing the table, I came straight to the real point of my visit. 'Will you buy a ticket in the sweepstake, Mrs. Morris?'

On her way to the kitchen, she called over her shoulder, 'What is it, Davy—Harvest Festival?'

'Not really,' I said, as off-hand as I could manage. 'Irish Sweepstake.'

You would have thought I had made a lewd suggestion. She swung around, cup and saucer going one way, plate the other, and all shattering on the polished tile floor. 'David Price! That's gambling! Whatever would your father say?' Ebenezer Chapel was written all over her horror-stricken face.

'It's no more gambling than the Harvest Festival draw, Mrs. Morris,' I argued, going on my knees to help pick up the pieces. There seemed little chance of convincing her so I came up with my trump card. 'I've sold a half share in a ticket to 'Cap'n Once'. He would like you to buy the other half.'

She looked up, her eyes making daggers. 'Captain Evans to you, boy! Don't they teach you manners at Llangarron?'

There was a flush in her cheeks that was more than just anger, so I pressed on. 'There's several thousand pounds for first prize, Mrs. Morris, and if Cap'n . . . er . . . Evans wins, he'll only spend the money on some old boat or something. Now, if you buy the other half of his ticket, perhaps . . .' I left the shop with another ten shilling note in my pocket.

★　　　★　　　★　　　★

The summer went by with its usual speed and, once again, the gates of Llangarron clanged shut behind me for another term. The book of Irish Sweepstake tickets I handed back to Isaac Lewis untouched, except for the one ticket shared by 'Cap'n Once' and Angharad Morris. It wasn't until much later I found out that, simultaneously with my furtive sales campaign, my dear mother had been flitting from door to door peddling tickets for the Harvest Festival draw. In a place like Dinas Coch, there was no way I could win against the power of the Church.

Less than a month after my return to college, the impossible happened. The sole ticket representing Dinas Coch in the Irish Sweepstake not only drew a horse, but the horse was first past the post. Five thousand pounds! There was only one snag. I had forgotten to add the name of Angharad Morris to the ticket counterfoil when she had parted with her ten shillings. 'Cap'n Once' was a rich man and I was in trouble.

When I reluctantly returned to the village at half-term, the place was in turmoil. 'Cap'n Once' had gone to Cardigan to negotiate for a second-hand herring drifter and Angharad Morris was in Carmarthen consulting a solicitor.

For two days I lurked behind the vicarage gates, not daring to show my face in the village. But, when I heard that 'Cap'n Once' was returning with his new boat, I was on the quay waiting. You could smell the fish a mile before he came chugging into the harbour at the wheel of the saddest looking hulk this side of the knacker's yard. The unscrupulous men of Cardigan had done their work well.

'Cap'n Once' slammed the poor thing alongside the quay with his usual lack of finesse and called up to me, "What do you think of her, Davy? Beautiful, isn't she?'

'It smells,' I said, holding my nose.

He shinned up the quay wall and stood looking down at his new acquisition with pride, obviously blissfully unaware of the stench. He caught my arm and pointed at the sagging deckhouse. 'Look, Davy! It's even got a stove and a sink for the washing up. Just like a house it will be. A good wash down is all she needs.'

I struggled to hide my embarrassment. 'How much did you pay?' I asked, dreading his answer.

'One thousand nine hundred pounds.' He gave a short, contemptuous laugh. 'Those Cardies do think they are clever. Beat them down from two thousand five hundred, I did.'

I let out a sigh of relief. 'Thank the Lord for that! You've still got enough left to pay Angharad Morris her share of the winnings.'

He scratched his three-day growth of beard and gave me a sly look. 'Now . . . I don't know about that, Davy,' he said hesitantly. 'I went to see one of those solicitors myself in Cardigan. The law says the money is all mine.'

I put my head in my hands. 'She'll kill me when she gets back,' I said miserably.

In reply I got a slap on the back that all but sent my flying into the water below. 'Don't you worry, Davy,' he laughed. 'Thought of a plan, I have. Five thousand pounds will get me two birds for the price of one, so to speak. Now, listen to me, boyo . . .'

I listened and my spirits rose.

I went to see Angharad as soon as she returned from Carmarthen. No tea and scones this time. Just black looks and, 'What have you got to say for yourself, David Price?' She made no move to allow me into her shop.

Shamefaced, I scuffed my heels on her doormat. 'I'm sorry, Mrs. Morris,' I began.

She froze me with a look. 'Sorry, nothing! It was all arranged between you and Owain Evans, wasn't it?' She put her hands on her hips and tossed her head. 'What did those Cardies sell him? A load of old rubbish, I'll be sure!'

I must have shown suitable repentance for, with a snort, she opened the door wide and motioned me inside. 'Ah, well . . .,' she said, 'what's done is done. Inside with you and I'll make some tea.'

As we sat facing each other across the table, the brown china teapot and a plate of scones between us, I was silent, wondering how to lead into my reason for coming.

She made the opening for me. 'Is that silly old fool serious about sailing around the world?' she asked.

I nodded. 'Very serious. Being 'Cap'n Once' is a terrible weight for him to bear. He says he will do it to prove the people of Dinas Coch wrong.'

'Silly old fool!' she said again, but now there were tears in her eyes.

My confidence was increasing. 'Marry him, Angharad,' I said in a voice fit to charm the birds out of the trees. 'Then, half the prize money will be legally yours, anyway. And, perhaps you could talk him into doing just a short trip—across to Ireland and back, say.'

I was soon into my second plate of scones and Angharad was singing softly in the kitchen.

They were married in the spring, when the hillsides were aflame with yellow gorse. Soon afterwards, the *Lady Angharad*, as the old Cardigan drifter had been re-named, sported chintz curtains in the wheelhouse and cane furniture on the after deck. The great voyage was on. It was my secret belief the 'Cap'n Once' had been busy with the madeira bottle again.

Two years later, on a quiet autmn afternoon, the *Lady Angharad* re-entered Dinas Coch harbour to a tumultuous welcome. Captain 'Round the World' Evans manouvered his ship skilfully alongside the quay then, with his head held high, stepped ashore to accept the accolades of the villagers. On his heels, with a tan fit to shame a South Sea Island maiden, came Angharad Evans, a beautiful baby girl cradled in her arms.

THE PASSING OF BLACK BEN

Close southwards of the rolling Preseli Hills, in the county of Pembrokeshire, there is a place where the clean, sharp smell of salt water mingles with the scent of meadowsweet and winter fogs roll up the valley from the sea to draw ghostly curtains around the cattle grazing in the fields. The tiny hamlet of Castlefach lies in a foreign, half-anglicised enclave of Wales and was once, albeit unwillingly, the seat of Roger of Montgomery, whose Norman echelons reigned supreme for more than twenty bloody and destructive years. It was also the birthplace and home of a Welsh seaman whose prowess and infamy reverberated around the world in an age when the booming staysail and the whetted cutlass conquered all.

Today, Castlefach is no more than a dozen sturdy houses which cluster in an orderly fashion around an English-style village green formed by the uneasy convergence of three narrow roads. On the south side of the green slumbers a small, lichen-encrusted 14th century church, dedicated to a long-forgotten St. Brynach, who once took counsel with the angels on nearby Carn Ingli. To the north squats the white-faced *King's Arms*, with its huge inglenook fireplace and smoke-blackened beams; a meeting place for farmers and sailors for more than three centuries. Close by, in the shade of a towering, broad-leaved sycamore, lie the crumbling ruins of a small, stone-built cottage. A rough-hewn monument of granite proclaims that here, in 1682, was born one Benedict Jones, 'pirate and gentleman'.

★ ★ ★ ★

His Britannic Majesty's ship *Challenger*, a 26-gun frigate of 360 tons, lolled idly in the low equatorial swell. The early morning off-shore breeze was light, barely enough to take the creases out of the three-master's square-rigged sails. Although the sun had lately risen, the heat was oppressive,

19

bringing sweat freely to the bare backs of the seamen holy-stoning the ship's teakwood decks under the eye of a tight-lipped boatswain's mate. Overhead, the sky was pale blue and cloudless, presaging the real heat of the day yet to come.

Astern of the ship's dribbling wake, the thickly wooded hump of Cape Lopez, westernmost point of the French Congo, quickly cast off its shadows as the sun accelerated in its daily climb to the zenith. Spiralling lazily into the air, the smoke from a dozen or so cooking fires reached high into the shimmering sky. The hollow thud of a drum tapping out an urgent and insistent message, carried faintly across the water. This was rich slave country and the presence of a ship the size of the *Challenger* was sufficient to put the locals on their guard.

'Sail to larboard!' came a thin cry from high in the war-ship's rigging. Far out on the slowly hardening horizon, a tiny cluster of white canvas gave warning of the approach of another ship. As the distance shortened and a dark hull rose above the horizon, it could be seen that the other vessel was also a three-master and coasting up from the south on a con-verging course with the *Challenger*.

Captain Dudley Hood lowered his telescope and shut it with a decisive snap. 'Well . . . what do you make of her, Lieutenant?' he grunted, turning to the young officer at his side.

Lieutenant William Foley spread his thin legs well apart and steadied his glass against the shrouds. After several inept attempts at focusing, he removed his eye from the lens. 'It looks like a . . . er . . . another ship, sir,' he offered without conviction.

Hood exploded. 'Of course it's another ship, you fool! What kind of a ship, man? Fishing boat? Ship-of-the-Line? Friend? Enemy? Come on, Foley! For once in your miserable life make a sensible report.'

Foley's pale face reddened with confusion and he fumbled the telescope to his eye again. Passable seaman though he might be, his rapid promotion engineered through family connections had left him woefully short on experience. He studied the other ship carefully before speaking. 'Could be a Portuguese slaver, sir,' he said with more confidence.

'Good God, man!' Hood spat out impatiently. 'You wouldn't know a Portuguese slaver if she hoisted her flag in your blasted drawing room.' He pointed a thick finger. 'If you'd open your eyes, Lieutenant, you'd see that is without doubt the *Guinea Queen*—the ship we've been chasing for these past two months.'

Lieutenant Foley blanched. The *Guinea Queen* was the flagship of Benedict Jones—Black Ben—the swarthy Welshman who, over a period of four years, had carved out a name for himself as the most successful and elusive pirate the world had ever known. Recently, having brought all commercial shipping in the Caribbean to a virtual standstill, the buccaneer had turned his attention exclusively to the Gulf of Guinea. Rampaging up and down the coast, from the mangrove-fringed shores of Sierra Leone to the steaming creeks of Equatorial West Africa, he had waged a systematic campaign of murder and pillage against shipping and trading posts for almost half a year. So efficient and persistent had been his attacks that the enraged British merchants on the coast had lobbied Parliament for protection. The *Challenger*, hastily pulled away from her routine Mediterranean patrol, had been the answer to their plea.

Not that the warship's arrival had seemingly had any great effect on Black Ben's activities. The *Challenger* had, in fact, developed the unfortunate knack of always running second in a two-horse race. Whenever Black Ben struck, the *Challenger* was never far below the horizon, but always too late to bring the pirate to book. The merchants ashore had become incensed and goaded into further political activity. As for the men of the *Challenger*, bitter frustration had been added to the normal discomforts of life in a man-of-war. Most recently, they had followed in Black Ben's bloody wake, witnessing the results—and always only the results—of his sacking of ports along the entire 3000 mile length of the Guinea Coast. Sherbro, Sestos, Axim and Elmina had felt the pirates' scourge in quick succession and without hope of retaliation. His most impudent and recent excess had been an attack on the great slaving port of Whydah, in the Niger Delta, where he had surprised and sunk no less than eleven ships waiting off the port. Angry and distraught traders had reported to the *Challenger*'s commander that Black Ben, after sacking the Royal Africa Company's post ashore and making off with a small fortune in gold dust, had callously battened down the hatches of the slave ships and set fire to them. Hundreds of slaves had been burned alive.

Foley pulled himself together. 'Shall I . . . er . . . beat to quarter's, sir?'

'Do that, Mister Foley,' Hood answered crisply, satisfied that Black Ben was at last within his grasp.

While the drums rattled and the decks of the *Challenger* came alive to the slap of bare feet, Hood studied his adversary. She was, as he well knew, the ex-Royal Africa Company's frigate *Harcourt*, captured by Black Ben in a bloody fight off Cape Palmas. She was a match in size and speed for the *Challenger* and there had been reliable reports that, after her capture, the *Harcourt*'s armament had been increased from 26 to 40 guns. If this was true, then the *Guinea Queen*, as Black Ben had impudently re-named her, was a formidable enemy: one to be tackled with extreme caution.

Hood was familiar with his opponent's strength but puzzled by her behaviour. The *Guinea Queen* was dawdling along close-hauled on the starboard tack, making a course at a rough angle of 45 degrees with that of the *Challenger*. Her guns had not been run out, nor was she flying her ensign; all of which led Hood to suspect that his own ship had not yet been recognised for what she was. Yet he knew the *Guinea Queen* was no run-of-the-mill pirate ship, most of whom kept a poor lookout. Black Ben was ex-Navy and reputed to run a very tight ship. There was something very suspicious about the whole thing. It could well be, Hood decided, a clever subterfuge needing to be matched with subterfuge.

Hood swung on his heel. 'Lieutenant Foley!'

Foley came aft at a trot. 'Yes, sir?'

'We'll run up the French flag, if you please.'

Foley stopped dead in his tracks, bewilderment spreading over his young face. 'The French flag, sir? Our colours . . .'

Hood cut him short with a roar. 'Our colours, be damned! This is no time to play the game by the rules, Mister.' He turned and pointed to the other ship. 'Given the chance, that ship can outsail and outfight us any day. I don't intend to give her that chance.'

The lieutenant took a step backwards. 'But sailing under false colours, sir . . .'

Hood's florid face was mottled with rage, his voice low and menacing. 'Mister Foley . . . Black Ben is an enemy of the Crown. For four years he has waged a murderous, destructive war against shipping on both sides of the Atlantic. The man is a plague and there will be no freedom of the seas until he is dead. I mean to put an end to that impudent Welshman before this day is out. Is that understood?'

Foley squared his shoulders. 'Yes, sir,' he answered quietly.

Satisfied, Hood nodded. 'Right! Hoist the French flag and we'll see if our friend Black Ben takes the bait.'

★   ★   ★   ★

Captain Benedict Jones—Black Ben, as he was known to his enemies—was at breakfast in the great cabin of the *Guinea Queen*. Before him on the polished rosewood dining table—a luxury bequeathed to him by the cabin's previous, and late, blue-coated occupant—was a plate piled high with Jones' favourite salmagundi, slices of cured fish and onions, boiled together and garnished with beetroot. He ate heartily, pausing from time to time to drink from a huge mug of steaming tea. Incongruous in a pirate ship, perhaps, but very much in line with Jones's naval background, his personal servant, Huw Pugh, hovered at his elbow throughout the meal.

Pugh was a small, shrivelled-up man with tight, curly hair, white as a fleece, and a black patch over his right eye. Ironically, he had lost the eye and acquired several lasting scars about his body in a brush with pirates while serving in an East Indiaman some twenty years previously. Unlike many of his shipmates, he had survived to return to his native Castle-fach. There, he had lived miserably, half-starved, an outcast and an object of ridicule until Benedict Jones had arrived to recruit a crew. Pugh, growing old and without hope, had offered his services at once. Much to his surprise and joy, he was accepted. Benedict Jones was a man not without compassion and ever mindful of his own beginnings.

Born without any vestige of privilege, his father a pressed seaman deserted from the King's Navy, his mother the illegitimate daughter of an Irish gypsy, Benedict Jones had tasted the extremities of poverty in his youth. His father had been re-taken by the Press Gang a few days after Benedict's birth, never to return. At thirteen, the young Ben had hied himself off to sea, volunteering for the very service which had so callously snatched his father. In doing so, he exchanged purgatory ashore for a similar state afloat. Life at sea in the seventeenth century was hard indeed. For those of the lower deck, among which Benedict was numbered, accommodation was any place a man could lay his head. The food was execrable, water always tightly rationed and the discipline total and unchallengeable. The boatswain's cane was used constantly and sadistically; at a captain's whim, a man could be flogged at the gratings, flogged around the fleet and, if the offence warranted it under King's Regulations, hung from the yard-arm. Even ashore, Jack fared little better. Pimps, prostitutes and footpads stood in line to relieve him of his hard-earned guineas. Once cast aside by them, penniless and sodden with drink, he was once more easy prey for the marauding Press Gangs. Then the whole degrading round would begin again.

Fortunately, the rigours of his early life in Castlefach had amply prepared Jones for the Draconian extremes of the seventeenth century Navy. He silently suffered the abuse, the beatings, the discomfort and the privation, all the while applying his agile mind to learning the skills of navigation and seamanship. By the time he was thirty, he was a sailing master; a short, wide-shouldered man who exuded an air of unassailable authority. Unlike most seamen of his day, who affected thick beards and long, unkept hair, Jones was clean shaven and wore his Celtic curls cut close to his skull. As a sailing master, he ranked as a junior lieutenant in the Navy's hierarchy but, being the son of a lowly seaman, he could expect to go no further. The senior ranks were reserved exclusively for the gentry.

While Jones was stoically enduring life in the King's ships, there were others who were reaping rich rewards from their seafaring activities. This was the Golden Age of piracy, when men like Edward Blackbeard Teach, Long Ben Avery and Calico Jack Rackam were ruthlessly plundering the seaboards of America and Africa. The ships of these men, and their lesser contemporaries, were, day in day out, returning to their bases loaded to the gunwales with booty. It was not uncommon for a man who signed the Pirate Articles to make as much as £3000 out of a year's voyaging. To the habitually poorly paid British seaman, this was wealth untold, equalling the annual incomes of many of the landowning aristocracy of their country. Little wonder they flocked to serve under the Jolly Roger.

With characteristic determination, Jones quit the Navy at the age of thirty five and joined up with the Brethren of the Coast. Such was his ability that he made an instant success of this, his second career. Within six months, he was commanding his own ship and, within a year, holding sway over a fleet of pirate ships. His fearless and brilliantly successful attacks on shipping in the Caribbean soon earned him the name Black Ben. By the beginning of 1720, his activities had brought all merchant shipping in the Caribbean to a complete halt. He then shifted his sphere of action to the West Coast of Africa with equal success.

In the late spring of 1721, Jones returned briefly to Pembrokeshire. He came not to boast of his achievements in the field of buccaneering—although he might well have done so—but to recruit what he had long envisaged would be his ideal crew. He wanted Welshmen, sturdy, resourceful men who would, without question, obey the commands of their Welsh master. The careful distribution of the precious stones he brought with him and the promise of more to be won, brought forward a surfeit of willing recruits and, for some strange reason, many of them came over the Preseli Mountains from the Gwaun Valley.

Pushing aside the empty plate, Jones leaned back in his chair with a sigh of satisfaction. 'That was first class, Huw. Another pot of tea now, if you please.'

Huw Pugh bobbed and gave a toothless smile. 'A nice jug of wine would do you better, Cap'n.'

Jones came forward in his chair and slammed the table with the flat of his hand. 'One-eyed bastard!' he roared. 'It is tea I will have. You can keep your old wine.'

Pugh muttered grumpily as he hobbled over to the locker where he kept the brass samovar constantly hot. He could never come to terms with his master's addiction to bitter tea. Rum and wine were real pirates' drinks.

'Just rots your stomach, this,' Pugh grumbled, banging down the heavy china mug in front of the captain.

'Now there's a drink for you,' Jones enthused, stirring two ounces of rough brown sugar into the steaming, amber liquid. 'No hangovers for me like the rest of you scum are suffering this morning.'

Pugh showed his gums. This was a game he played with his captain on many a morning. 'You don't know what you're missing, Cap'n. Lovely drop of wine that was last night. Not that I made a pig of myself like some people,' he added quickly.

Jones sipped his tea with appreciation and pondered on the problems created by strong drink. Although he was himself a strict teetotaler, he was able to understand the craving his men had for drink. A pirate's life was not all one round of exhilarating battle and prize-taking. In between the successful forays, there were long periods of boredom. Food and water were often short, dysentry, venereal disease and the many prevalent fevers of the day took a heavy toll of life. Rum—and in its absence, wine—were the pirate's great comforters. They consumed them in great quantities to celebrate their bloody conquests, sometimes in action to supplement their courage but mostly between raids to relieve the terrible boredom they suffered. Then, if the drink was to hand, they invariably drank themselves insensible and stayed that way until it was once more necessary to earn a dishonest penny.

Throughout his buccaneering career, Jones had striven to moderate and control the consumption of alcohol in his ships. For much of the time, his efforts had been in vain. Many of the ships plundered carried large quantities of drink and, a pirates life being what it was, for his men, the numbing oblivion provided by the drink was an essential part of the daily round. He had recruited his Pembrokeshire crew, confident that, for once, he would be able to run a sober ship. While these men were no angels, they were God-fearing and, in the main, teetotal. For a while it seemed that his hopes had been realised. Except for developing an insatiable appetite for the charms of black women, the men had behaved well. Then, with the capture of a French merchantman deep-laden with casks of wine for the Ivory Coast, things had begun to go very wrong. The simple Welshmen had supped the wine like water, reeling from one drunken orgy to another. The burning of the slaves at Whydah had been the culmination of a week of drinking, with Jones the only sober man on board and powerless to intervene. Now they were drinking to forget the dying screams of those black innocents.

★   ★   ★   ★

The mug was again empty and Jones motioned for a refill. 'What state are they in this morning, Huw?' he asked thoughtfully.

Pugh sniffed. 'Every one of them with heads as big as buckets—and serve them right, too!' He poured the tea slowly and deliberately, filling the mug to the brim.

As Jones nodded his thanks and raised the mug to his lips, there was the slap of bare feet on the ladder and the heavy canvas curtain covering the doorway to the great cabin was pulled roughly aside. The bleary-eyed figure of the quartermaster Caradog Evans lurched through. 'Ship on the starboard bow, Cap'n!' he reported breathlessly.

Jones lowered his mug and stared at the swaying man contemptuously. 'Well, Caradog Evans?' he said coldly. 'What do you want me to do about it?'

Bewildered at his captain's apparent disinterest, Evans worried at the short stubble on his chin with a grubby hand. 'Don't know, Cap'n,' he mumbled at last. 'It's just that Mog Griffiths, the sailing master, told me to tell you . . .'

'And what else did Mog Griffiths tell you?' Jones interrupted. 'Did he tell you what kind of a ship this is and how far off?'

Evans shook his head. 'No, Cap'n. Mog said . . .'

'*Diawl!*' Jones swore, kicking back his chair and rising. 'Tell Mister Mog Griffiths from me—a proper report next time. No half measures, mind!'

With a hurt expression on his blotched face, Evans backed out of the cabin, carefully drawing the curtain closed behind him.

When the man had gone, Jones sat down again. 'Are they in a fit state for a fight, Huw?' he asked, holding out his mug for replenishment.

Pugh took the mug and refilled it at the hissing samovar. 'Hardly, Cap'n,' he said with a low chuckle. 'Up all night they were, drinking and singing.' He shook his head sadly. 'Acting like animals, too. No one to keep them in their place, see.'

Jones ignored the implied rebuke. 'What about Mog Griffiths and Bryn Thomas, the gunner?'

'Oh . . . they're sober enough, I suppose.' Pugh put his head on more side and regarded the captain quizzically. 'You're not thinking of trying to take this ship, are you?'

'I might,' Jones answered thoughtfully, tackling his fresh mug of tea.

Pugh pulled a face. 'Bloody foolish, if you ask me.'

'I'm not asking you, Huw Pugh,' Jones said, glancing up as the unsteady figure of Caradog Evans appeared once more at the doorway. 'Well . . . Evans?' he asked.

Evans entered and touched his fringe. 'Mog Griffiths said to tell you she's about three miles off and converging and she's hoisted the French colours. He says do you want to run up the jack now, Cap'n?' Evans was referring to Black Ben's personal Jolly Roger, which depicted not the usual skull and crossbones, but a skeleton being savaged by a fire-breathing dragon.

Jones shook his head. 'Time enough to hoist the jack when she's in range of our cannon. Tell Mog to take a reef in his drawers and stand fast.'

Evans hesitated. 'You're not coming on deck to see, Cap'n?'

This brought Huw Pugh hobbling forward, growling like a faithful guard dog. 'You heard what the Cap'n said, mun!' He gave Evans a shove, propelling him backwards through the doorway. When the man had gone stumbling up the ladder to the deck, Pugh turned to his master with a sly smile of antici-pation. 'Shall I lay your clothes out, Cap'n?'

Jones took a long swig at his tea before answering. His voice betrayed little interest. 'It's only an old French slaver, Huw. Full cargo of black hams. Not much we could do with them.' As he spoke, he recalled the screaming blacks of Whydah, chained below decks and roasting alive. He frowned.

Pugh licked his lips. 'Might be some women, Cap'n,' he said, his one eye gleaming.

Jones snorted. 'I should have thought you were a bit old for that sort of thing, Huw Pugh! Besides, you know my rules about women on the ship.' As a threat to the efficiency of his ship, Jones rated women only second to drink. Apart from the ever present risk of the incurable pox, women were just another debauchery that sapped a man's strength, dulled his brain.

Pugh was embarrassed. 'Bit of womanflesh now and again never a did a man any harm, Cap'n,' he mumbled.

Coming to his feet, Jones began to stride up and down the narrow confines of the cabin, his head bent to avoid the low deckhead beams. 'You're as bad as the rest of them, Huw Pugh,' he grumbled. 'A bottle of rum and a pair of fat tits is all you want. You disgust me!'

The small man stood his ground. 'I know you're not one for the drink, Cap'n, but you're married and you know what it's like to have a woman in your bed.' Pugh seemed on the point of slobbering. '*Diawch*, Cap'n . . . you wouldn't deny . . .'

Jones stopped his pacing and rounded on Pugh angrily. 'Don't you bring my wife into this, you disgusting little slob!' The beautiful Gaenor Morgan, wedded and bedded by Jones on his brief stay in Castlefach some nine months previously, was high on a pedestal, her image sacrosanct. 'I'll not have her lumped with the black trash you're lusting after,' Jones raged on. 'Poxed up to the eyebrows these women are . . . or didn't you know that? It's bad enough I have to fight my ship with a bunch of drunken sots. I don't want the pox among you as well. Rot away before my eyes, you will. The lot of you won't be fit to paddle a canoe up the Calabar River, let alone get this ship back to Wales.' He halted in front of Pugh. 'That gold you've got stowed away in your seachest wouldn't be worth a tuppenny damn then, would it, Huw Pugh? All the gold in Africa can't cure the pox and you can't walk home.'

The talk of the vile, creeping disease and, more so, the implied threat to his share of the *Guinea Queen*'s booty, brought Pugh out in a cold sweat. In those precious ounces of yellow dust lay his only hope of fulfillment of his dream of long standing—his own farm in Pembrokeshire. Ten acres would be enough; a small herd of cows, a few pigs, chickens scratching in the yard and, most important, the big-breasted Annie Hughes sharing his bed in the cosy farmhouse he would build. The captain was right. To put such a future at risk was unthinkable.

The clump of hurrying boots on the ladder brought both captain and servant back to reality. Mog Griffiths, sailing master, his remaining grey hairs forming a saintly fringe around his shining skull, pushed aside the door curtain and entered the cabin. There was a worried frown on his face. 'We're in trouble, Cap'n,' he announced, without preamble.

Jones returned to the table and swilled down the last of his tea. 'Well . . . Mog?' he said coolly, studying the pattern of the leaves in the bottom of the mug.

The sailing master stood with his feet well apart, swaying easily with the movement of the ship. 'She's no Frenchman, Cap'n. I think we'll have to fight.'

'And why do you think that, Mog?' Jones asked quietly. 'You know I never fight except on my own terms. Frenchman or not, we'll let her go. The men are in no fit state to fight.'

Griffiths shook his head. 'It's not a case of letting her go, Cap'n. She's coming after us. She's a British man-of-war.'

Hugh Pugh drew in a sharp breath but Jones laughed. 'It's those old eyes of yours playing you up, Mog. There's not a British warship within a thousand miles of us.'

Griffiths shifted his feet uncomfortably. 'Begging your pardon, Cap'n. John Roderick, the helmsman, says she's the *Challenger*. He sailed in her as a pressed man.'

Jones gave a short laugh. 'Well, I'll be damned! My old friend Captain Dudley Hood, eh?' He ruffled his curls in a strangely boyish manner. 'Then we are in for a fight, Mog.' He turned to Pugh, who was polishing the table in long lazy strokes, one ear cocked. 'Lay out my silks, Huw. Pistols well primed, mind. I'm going on deck.'

Despite his light clothing, Jones broke out into an immediate sweat when he reached the deck. The sun, now high in the sky, was a searing ball of fire. Shading his eyes, he swept the horizon, point by point. Satisfied he was not being drawn into a trap, he turned his attention to the other vessel. With her white sails set taut and her brown-painted hull gleaming wet in the spray from her bow wave, she was under two miles off and holding confidently on a deliberate converging course. Although she was a square-rigged three-master of much the same type as the *Guinea Queen*, she was of more sturdy build. To Jones' practised eye this marked her as a Chatham ship and he knew without a second glance she was indeed the Royal Navy frigate *Challenger*. Her armament consisted of 26 12-pounder cannon and she carried a crew of 195, including a detachment of marines, all crammed into her 120-foot hull. She was a formidable enemy, commanded by a man Jones had come both to hate and respect. Captain Dudley Hood, a bulldog-like adversary, had once chased the notorious Edward England's *Fancy* 5000 miles across the Indian Ocean, only giving up when the wily England had slipped through the Sunda Strait and found sanctuary among the islands of the Java Sea. The same Dudley Hood had been equally tenaciously shadowing the *Guinea Queen* since she had left the Sherbro River 1600 miles to the west. Now Hood had found his quarry at last and there was no place for Jones to run.

Jones shrugged and turned to survey the state of his own ship. During the five weeks spent careening the *Guinea Queen* in the mosquito-infested creeks of the Sherbo River, he had lost ten men to malaria and blackwater fever. Ten of his best men—the very backbone of his crew. Trystan James, carpenter, a worker of miracles with an adze, Owain Williams, the helmsman who would follow a star to the edge of the world, Rhys Mostyn, master gunner, Henry Owens, sailmaker and six others dying so fast that Jones was hard pressed to put a name to them. They had all been good Castle-fach men, born within the sound of the bells of St. Brynach's, sparing with the wine and faithful to the women they had left behind them. Now, Jones was left with a total crew of 80, most of them lying about the deck sleeping off the effects of their drunken carousal of the previous night. Mog Griffiths, the sailing master, was sober enough, to be sure. The same went for Bryn Thomas, newly promoted to gunner, and a dozen or so men Griffiths had gathered about him ready to tend sails and man guns if it came to a fight. The rest were so much ballast.

Striding to the weather rail, Jones stood watching the *Challenger*, assessing the threat she posed to his ship. Assuming he held the *Guinea Queen* to her present course, she would be within range of the frigate's guns in less than an hour. At any other time, he would have had no hesitation in joining action. The *Guinea Queen* mounted almost twice as many guns as the *Challenger* and, broadside for broadside, the fight could have had only one conclusion; another victory for Black Ben. Now, with the great majority of his crew stupid with drink, Jones knew the odds against him were too great. Turning from the rail abruptly, he hailed the sailing master. 'Mog! Mog Griffiths!'

Griffiths came at a shambling run. 'Cap'n?'

Jones made a gesture of dismissal towards the *Challenger*.

'No fight for us today, Mog. Put her about and we'll make a run for it.'

The relief flooding across the sailing master's face eased ten years off his age. Mog Griffiths, conscious that, for him, time was running out and with an agonising ache in his heart for his beloved Pembrokeshire, had no stomach for the fight.

★   ★   ★   ★

On the tense quarterdeck of the *Challenger*, Lieutenant Foley bubbled with suppressed excitement. 'She's putting about, sir!' he shrilled. 'She's running!'

Captain Dudley Hood turned to his 1st lieutenant with a look of stern disapproval. 'I am quite aware of that, Mister Foley. Pirates always run, they don't fight. That is work for his Majesty's Navy. Now stand by to go about.'

'Are we . . . er . . . giving chase, sir?'

'Good God, man! Of course we are. Now get on with it before Black Ben disappears over the horizon.'

Hood strode purposefully to the weather side of the quarter deck and began to pace quickly up and down. 'Heaven preserve me from thick-headed, spineless privilege officers!' he muttered under his breath. Lieutenant Foley was a nephew of Rear Admiral Sir Humphrey Foley, commander-in-chief of the Mediterranean Squadron—a man who held considerable sway with their Lordships. Much as Hood despised the young Foley, he could ill afford to push him too far.

Oblivious to the importance of his family connections, Foley raised his speaking trumpet. 'Man the braces!' he roared, his voice beginning bass but rising to an unfortunate girlish shriek. 'Prepare to wear ship!'

On deck, there were a few sly grins and ribald gibes but the *Challenger*'s men were acutely conscious of the forbidding figure of their commander striding the quarterdeck. 'Flogger' Hood was not one to tolerate insubordination, however invoked. With only an almost imperceptible dragging of their heels, all hands ran to lay hold of the braces. At Foley's hesitant word of command, the helm was put down, ropes surged squealing through the blocks and, as the wind came astern, the *Challenger*'s full spread of canvas was squared off to take maximum advantage of the following wind. In a stiff breeze, the warship would expect to make 14 knots on this running tack but, with the wind now light and fretful, Hood would have to be content with a modest 7 or 8 knots.

'Lose a capful of wind and I'll have you flogged!' Hood roared at the perspiring helmsman who, with the muscles of his bare back rippling, was making fine adjustments to his course. Although the *Guinea Queen*'s manoeuvre to put the wind astern and run had been a ragged performance, the unexpectedness of the move had already increased the distance between the two ships by half a mile. Hood had no illusions about this being anything but a long chase. The pirate ship, as would be expected of an ex-Royal Africa Company's frigate, was a good sailer and, in theory, every bit as fast as the *Challenger*. The deciding factor might well be the weight of the extra 14 guns the *Guinea Queen* was reported to be carrying. Only time would tell; and Captain Dudley Hood had plenty of that.

As the *Guinea Queen*'s sails billowed in the stern wind and her wake curved away from the still close-hauled *Challenger*, Benedict Jones re-appeared on deck dressed for battle. He was, in spite of his sober mode of life, an incurable dandy in the matter of clothes. He wore now, as he always did in action, coat and breeches of crimson damask, black tricorn hat topped by a huge red ostrich plume and black leather shoes with gold buckles. A large diamond cross, suspended around his neck on a gold chain as thick as a horse's halter, flashed back a thousand facets of fire at the burning sun. Draped across his shoulders, a silk sling acted as holster for two brace of ornate 14-bore pistols. At his hip, he carried a regulation 27-inch Naval boarding cutlass, the only sober thing on his person.

Mog Griffiths took off his shapeless canvas hat and scratched his bald head. '*Duw*, Cap'n,' he rumbled with half a smile on his face, 'I can never understand why you wear those clothes. A blind gunner couldn't miss in a rainstorm.'

Jones shrugged and worked his broad-bladed cutlass in and out of its scabbard, testing its availability. 'If those boyoes over there have a mind to shoot me, Mog,' he said, indicating the *Challenger*, 'then it is the Lord's will. One thing they'll never do to Black Ben is to hang him up to dry like they did to William Kidd.' Almost twenty years before, Kidd, another naval officer turned pirate, had been hanged at Wapping and his body hung up in chains to decay. His death and grisly burial had little deterrent effect on the activities of the pirates but it had convinced men like Jones that capture must be avoided at all costs. For them, death in action was eminently preferable.

Mog Griffiths shook his head glumly and gestured astern. 'She's following us round, Cap'n. Going to give chase, for sure.'

Jones sheathed his sword with a final snap. 'Aye . . . she'll chase us all right, Mog. Hood won't give up until we're playing hide and seek down amongst the Antartic icebergs.'

The sailing master's frown deepened. 'You intend to run that far, Cap'n?'

Jones smiled. 'Don't you worry, Mog. We'll show him a clean horizon before dark. Then we'll double back to Sherbro as quick as you like. We need provisions and, more important, a new hunting ground.' He rubbed his chin thoughtfully. 'I have a mind to dip my hand in the Caribbean again, Mog.'

But Jones' confident forecast was not to hold good. As the sun crossed overhead and began its long descent into the clear sweep of the western horizon, the *Guinea Queen* lost ground with every hour that passed. Mog Griffiths, working like a man possessed, crowded on every square inch of canvas in the locker but to no avail. Relentlessly, the *Challenger* pulled closer yard by yard.

Captain Dudley Hood, a smile of anticipation on his face, paced the *Challenger*'s quarterdeck with a spring in his step. Passing his 1st lieutenant, who was anxiously gauging the distance between the two ships, he called out, 'You see, Mister Foley! Those extra guns are doing him no good. Too much weight for the ship . . . far too much!'

Foley nodded enthusiastically. 'Quite right, sir!' But within the shadowy corners of his mind there was no such conviction. The fight, when it came—and come it surely would—might be fearfully one-sided. The *Guinea Queen's* fire power was almost twice that of the *Challenger* and, if rumour was to be believed, Black Ben's gunners were very good. The young lieutenant was also clearly aware that pirates forced into a corner were at their most dangerous. They would ask for no quarter and give none, knowing full well that, for them, surrender and capture meant, at the very least, a lifetime of hard labour in the mines of the Gold Coast or, at worst, death by hanging at the yardarm of their victorious enemy.

Hood had seen the look of apprehension growing on his 1st lieutenant's face. Some sugar was needed to sweeten the coming draught, he decided. 'Pass the word, Mister Foley,' he growled amiably. 'There's a couple of thousand ounces of fine gold dust in that ship to be sure. Fair shares all round, tell the men.'

To Benedict Jones, gazing aft with his hands turning bloodless as his grip tightened on the taffrail, the inevitability of approaching death was obvious. The naval ship was now less than a mile astern and inching nearer with the stealthy tenacity of a stalking jaguar. Jones bit his lip and roundly cursed the extra guns fate had thrown his way in the Sherbro River. They were now a crushing liability, holding his ship back as surely as if she had a sea anchor streamed in her dwindling wake. Most of all, he cursed the state of his men, whose drink-sapped bodied were incapable of levering the surplus canon overboard. Very soon, they would be within range of the *Challenger's* bow-chaser. Hood would go for the *Guinea Queen's* sails first, patiently riddling them one by one, with every ball whittling another fraction of a knot off the pirate ship's speed. If Rhys Mostyn, the master gunner, had lived, Jones reflected bitterly, he would have been able to use the *Guinea Queen's* stern-chaser to equal effect, matching ball with ball and torn sail with torn sail. But the man was gone, his body rotting in the grey mud of the Sherbro River, along with the others. There was no man left, either drunk or sober, who could lay and shoot a long 9-pounder like Rhys Mostyn.

Grimly, Jones decided there was only one course of action open to him. Straightening up, he turned and strode purposefully to the forward end of the raised quarterdeck. Leaning on the rail, he surveyed the deck below him. For all the world, it resembled the scene outside a dockside tavern on the morning after an East Indiaman had made port. Men were lying in their own vomit, some with their heads in their hands and groaning, others still insensible with drink. Mog Griffiths and two of his sober men were hard at work with rope's ends and buckets of water in a desperate attempt to bring back life to the borderline cases. It was a hopeless task.

'Mog!' Jones called. 'Come up here.'

Looking up, Griffiths dropped his bucket and came up the ladder at a limping run. 'Yes, Cap'n?' he said breathlessly as he stumbled onto the quarterdeck.

Jones gripped the old man's shoulder and looked him in the eye. 'Can you manage a broadside, Mog? Just one. I'll go about and run down on her.'

Griffiths met his captain's eyes, doubt, anxiety and, finally, determination showing in the lines of his face. He worried at the grey bristles of his chin with the palm of his hand and looked astern, studying the King's ship with her now drum-tight sails and creaming bow wave. The situation was certainly bad enough to warrant what Black Ben had in mind. It could be done. A quick tack up into the wind and then run back down the *Challenger*'s starboard side before her captain could react to the surprise move. One punishing broadside from the twenty 12-pounders on the *Guinea Queen*'s starboard gundeck could cripple the naval ship.

The sailing master sucked at his teeth. 'One broadside, Cap'n—and then what? Do you intend to board her?' His voice had a worried edge to it.

Jones looked down at the chaos of the maindeck and shook his head. 'No, Mog. I fear we can muster no more than twenty men—and most of them half-drunk. Our only chance is to put one good broadside into that ship; bring down her masts, perhaps. Then we could make a run for it.'

A new hope dawned in Griffiths' eyes. He squared his shoulders. 'I'll give you a broadside, Cap'n—even if I have to lay every damned gun myself! You want me to hoist the jack now?' he added.

Jones nodded, 'Do that, Mog. And I want my band on the foc'sle playing. Put their heads under the pump if they need sobering up.'

The sailing master smiled to himself as he went down the ladder at a jerky run. When it came to a fight, Black Ben couldn't resist putting on a show. The fiddle, fife and drum of his personal band playing the ship into action well matched his grand, silken clothes.

Lieutenant Foley raised his telescope quickly when he saw the flag rise fluttering to the pirate ship's masthead. Bringing the square of bunting into sharp focus, he gave an involuntary shudder. It was Black Ben's own pirate jack, white on black, the skeleton and the fire-breathing dragon. 'He's hoisted his pirate jack, sir!' Foley called through his dry lips.

Captain Dudley Hood, standing with his legs well apart, folded his arms across his chest and laughed. 'Ho! So Black Ben means to fight, eh?' He beckoned Foley closer. 'This is where you earn those fat gold guineas the King pays you, Mister. I have a shrewd idea of what that man's going to attempt, so we'll be ready for him. Now listen carefully, lieutenant . . .'

In another hour, the two ships were 500 yards apart, with the *Challenger*'s long bowsprit reaching out for the *Guinea Queen*'s wallowing stern like a hungry rapier. With a sharp crack, the *Challenger*'s bow-chaser spoke and Jones, standing immobile by the helm of his ship, winced as the 9lb iron ball whistled high over his head to culminate in a harsh tearing sound as it found canvas in the topsails. It was time to act.

'Are you ready, Mog?' Jones called.

'When you are, Cap'n.' Griffiths answered firmly from the maindeck, where he had gathered his faithful few around him

'So be it then, Mog. Stand by!' Jones turned to the helmsman. 'Hard-a-larboard! Quick as you like, now!'

With a nod, the helmsman threw the whole weight of his body on the huge wheel, forcing the spokes over one by one.

Tackles screeched as they heaved the ship's great, iron-bound rudder to starboard, the rush of water on its paddle-like surface creating the necessary torque to set the bows canting; slowly at first, then with a rush. The way fell off the ship as the sails lost the wind and, for a brief moment, she was in irons. Then, with Mog Griffiths and his sweating, cursing men running the braces along the deck, the creaking yards followed the wind around. Carried by her own momentum and turning all the while, the ship crossed the wind and her sails were brought up close-hauled on the larboard tack. In minutes, the *Guinea Queen* had reversed her course and was gathering way to bear down on the starboard side of her pursuer.

'Man the starboard guns!' Jones roared through his speaking trumpet. 'Double shot, Mog!'

On the foc'sle deck, the three-piece band set up a jaunty Welsh air, stumbling over the notes but loud enough to set drunken heads stirring.

The two ships were now on parallel and opposing courses, approaching each other at a combined speed of 16 knots. In a very short space of time, they would be abreast, starboard to starboard, with only a narrow gulf of turbulent water separating them. When the simultaneous broadsides came, as come they must, the havoc wreaked in both ships would be devastating but, with the element of surprise in favour of the pirate ship, the *Challenger* would be dealt a death blow.

Mog Griffiths, pacing nervously behind his sparsely manned guns, searched for a long-forgotten prayer. He had loaded and primed every gun himself. It only remained for the men crouching beside the cannon to apply the slow match to the touchholes when the signal came. Slowed by the drink though they were, Griffiths was confident they could play their part.

On the quarterdeck, Jones calmly removed his tricorn hat and smoothed the red ostrich plume into shape. In turning to fight the *Challenger*, he was well aware of the horrendous risk he was taking. Under normal circumstances, given the *Guinea Queen*'s vast superiority in firepower, he would have stood off and reduced the other ship to a smoking hulk, if she dared to approach him. But desperate situations require desperate measures. He was without an experienced gunner and with only one man to a gun, instead of the usual crew of three. The rest of his crew were in no fit state to man guns, much less to form a boarding party capable of overwhelming the *Challenger*'s disciplined crew and sharpshooting marines. One single broadside it would have to be. If that failed to cripple the other ship, by the time the *Guinea Queen*'s severely depleted crew had re-loaded their guns— assuming they could do so—it would be all over.

Replacing his hat and seating it firmly, Jones unsheathed his cutlass and raised it high. 'Ready, Mog?' he called.

Black Ben's flamboyant gesture of defiance was never made. With the ships 50 yards apart, bow to bow, Dudley Hood ordered the *Challenger*'s helm hard to larboard. It was a dangerous move, which could have ended in a head-on collision, but it was timed to a split second. The *Challenger* still had the wind astern and her sails required a minimum of trimming. Without losing speed, she shot quickly across the advancing bow of the pirate ship. Hood then called for opposite helm and the *Challenger* resumed course, but now running down the *Guinea Queen*'s larboard side. Dudley Hood had neatly dealt himself a royal flush, for while his larboard guns were loaded and manned, those on the *Guinea Queen*'s larboard side were lashed in their inboard position, attended only by the drunken figures which used their carriages as pillows.

As one voice, the *Challenger*'s larboard battery roared, filling the air with spinning, whistling chain-shot. The helpless *Guinea Queen* shuddered under the impact of the hail of hot steel, her fore and main masts taking the main brunt of the broadside. Both masts were severed near to the deck and came crashing down, bringing with them a tangle of broken yards, blocks, rigging and torn canvas.

Mog Griffiths, hatless and bleeding, clawed his way up to the shambles of the quarterdeck. 'Cap'n!' he gasped. 'Cap'n . . . we're finished . . .!'

There was no answer from Jones. With his silken finery stained dark by his own blood, he lay at the foot of the compass binnacle, a spear-like splinter of wood piercing his heart. Benedict Jones, the peasant from Castlefach who had become Black Ben the greatest pirate the world had ever known, was dead.

A WOMAN'S PLACE

'Barefoot and pregnant, boyo. That's the only way to keep 'em in line.' Roly was giving forth on his favourite subject; women. Not that he had a grudge against women. He just liked them in their proper place which, knowing him, was in bed.

We were in my cabin knocking back gin and tonics. Not surprisingly, Roly's bottle was empty again so it *had* to be my place. Being chief officer of an old tramp like the *Welsh Princess* made booze just another occupational hazard for Roland Thomas. She was long overdue for scrapping and crewed by a bunch of dropouts from the Cardiff seamen's pool. Roly had, indeed, a heavy cross to bear.

'What time is he due on board?' Roly asked, characteristically changing his tack.

'Eh?' I said vaguely, having steeled myself for the inevitable debate on the merits and demerits of female emancipation.

'The new captain; Francis Honeywell. He's taking over today, you know.' There was more than a trace of bitterness in his voice. With old Captain Llewellyn having recently been carried ashore with the DT's, Roly had been hoping to take over command of the *Princess*. He was pushing forty, suitably qualified and, in spite of his fondness for the drink, a fine seaman. Yet he had been passed over.

'Francis . . .' Roly reflected into his empty glass. 'Bit of a pansy name for a skipper, isn't it?'

'Oh, I don't know,' I reasoned. 'Drake's name was Francis and he was no pansy.' I passed the gin bottle across and went to the fridge for more tonic. I was out. 'You'll have to get your own tonic if you want another drink,' I said over my shoulder.

Roly left the cabin muttering about the ridiculous price of tonic.

He hadn't been gone half a minute when the Second Engineer stuck his head through the doorway. 'Chief!' he croaked breathlessly. 'The Old Man's coming on board in about twenty minutes. ' There was a look of apprehension on his oil-streaked face.

'All right, lad. Don't upset yourself,' I said with more nonchalance than I felt. Captain Honeywell was, as yet, an unknown quantity. He could well be one of those sadists who enjoy making a chief engineer's life hell. The *Princess'* ancient Doxford engine was a full time job and I could well do without interference from a gentleman with scrambled egg on his cap—good navigator though he might be.

Roly was prising open a bottle of tonic as he re-entered my cabin. 'They're coming to sea now, you know,' he said.

I held up my glass. 'Who's coming to sea?' I couldn't follow his line of thinking at all.

He carefully measured tonic into my glass before replying. 'Bloody women, boyo! The *Welsh Duke's* got a female 3rd Mate and, only last week, Harry Parker on the *Consort* had two girl cadets dumped on him.' He took a long, thoughtful pull at his drink. 'I tell you, Bill, this Woman's Lib thing has gone too far.'

I took a positive line. 'They wouldn't dare put women on this ship, Roly. She's too old and, besides, we haven't got the facilities.'

'Facilities?' he asked with a frown.

'You know . . . showers and things.' The *Princess* had only two showers between ten officers, which often turned bathtime into a naked rugby scrum.

Roly leaned forward and decanted more of my gin into his glass. 'That wouldn't worry them,' he grunted. 'More than likely they'll be in the shower with you scrubbing your back. It's liberated these women are, don't forget.'

'Well here's one that wouldn't object to that,' I said with a laugh.

He gave me a pitying look. 'Get your mind above your navel, boyo. There's more to it than sex.'

'Nothing wrong with a bit of sex,' I countered. 'At least, you didn't seem to think so last night.' Roly had left the pub with his arm around a young widow who looked fit to eat him. It was six in the morning before he got back to the ship.

'That was different. There's a time and a place, you know,' he mused with a far-off look in his eyes. The widow must have been very accommodating. 'It's not only a question of sex, Bill,' he went on. 'These women are after our jobs, yours and mine.'

'Aw, come off it, man!' I said with feeling. 'Can you imagine a woman in my job? I've spent most of the last week in the engineroom bilges up to my knees in stinking, black oil. And what about you? On Saturday night you sorted out a full scale riot in the crew mess with your bare hands. I don't see any woman chief officer doing that.'

'You've got a point there,' he conceded, rubbing his still bruised knuckles. 'But the trouble is they *think* they can do our jobs. Heard all about the Russians, they have. Half the Russian merchant navy is female and our lot think it's about time they got in on the act. What they don't realise is that most Russian birds are built like lumberjacks.'

'Don't I know it,' I said ruefully. 'I tried to get off with one in a boozer in Murmansk once. She broke two of my fingers when I put my hand on her knee.'

He interrupted my painful reminiscence. 'It's this Sex Discrimination Act the Labour Government passed. Got to employ women in any job now—it's the law. If some young bint trips up the gangway waving a Second Mate's ticket, then you've got no choice. She signs on as 3rd Mate, golden ringlets, frilly knickers and all.' He viewed the light through the bottom of his empty glass and gave a snort of disgust.

I offered the bottle and tried to reason. 'This is 1984, Roly. I don't like the idea any more than you but we can't fight it.'

He charged his glass and gave me a look usually reserved for small children and imbeciles. 'There's one sure way to fight it, boyo,' he said confidently. 'Keep 'em barefoot and pregnant. They soon forget all about Women's Lib then.'

A discreet knock at the door signalled the arrival of Brinley Evans, Chief Steward. 'The new captain requests your presence, gentlemen,' he announced in his sonorous voice.

Brinley had once been butler to Lord Trefgarne and would not have anyone forget it.

Our voices joined in one question, 'What's he like?'

'Unusual. Yes . . . rather unusual, I would say,' Brinley replied slyly. As he eased his large bulk back through the doorway, he added, 'I suggest you gentlemen attend to your appearance before you approach the new captain.'

His parting shot was not without justification. Roly and I were hardly paragons of dress. I was marginally the more presentable, but only because I spent most of my time in a boiler suit, while my uniform hung unused in the wardrobe. Roly, on the other hand, was a mess. His uniform had a slept-in look, as did his grubby, off-white shirt. Then there was his hair. Rampant baldness had set in on top and, in an attempt to compensate for this, he was assiduously cultivating the remaining healthy locks at the back and sides. This clashed with the uniform and, in his more sober moments, gave him the appearance of a trendy, down-at-heel, country vicar.

We arrived in front of the Old Man's door with jackets buttoned and ties straight; the best we could do at short notice. As Roly knocked, I nervously polished my shoes on the back of my trousers.

'Come in!' The voice was muffled but unmistakably feminine.

'*Diawch*! He's got his wife with him,' Roly groaned. 'That's all we need. A bloody interfering Mrs. Captain.'

Anxious to get the interview over, I opened the door and bundled him inside, still muttering. Once across the threshold, we came up short, rigid with shock. Seated behind the familiar oak desk was an attractive woman. Early thirties, I guessed, with short, dark hair and nicely proportioned curves. She wore a captain's uniform, complete with the four gold bands of rank.

She rose and came from behind the desk. My stunned mind was able to take in her neat, black skirt and a pair of legs which could well have graced the centrefold of one of the more expensive girlie magazines.

Roly seemed to be in the throes of an apoplectic fit. 'It's a bloody joke!' he gasped, his face turning bright red.

'No . . . not a joke,' the woman said coldly. Her voice was low pitched with only a trace of Welsh accent. South Pembrokeshire, I thought. And educated too.

She stood with her legs slightly apart, hands clasped behind her back, and regarded us with a look of extreme distaste. 'I am Captain Frances Honeywell,' she said crisply, almost challenging. 'I take it you are my senior officers?'

I felt called upon to answer for both of us, Roly having gone unnaturally quiet. 'William Marsh, Chief Engineer, sir . . . er . . . madam.' I managed to stammer out. 'And this is Roland Thomas, your chief Officer,' I added, indicating Roly.

'Mister Thomas seems to have lost his tongue,' she remarked, raising her perfectly groomed eyebrows at Roly. 'I do hope this is not a permanent affliction, Mister Thomas.'

Roly's face was chalk-white. I fancied I could see foam at the corners of his mouth. 'A flaming woman!' he spluttered at last, slowly coming out of shock.

Captain Holywell returned behind her desk and sat down. She shuffled some papers before looking up. When she did, there was a flush of colour in her cheeks. 'Yes, Mister Thomas,' she said quietly. 'I am a woman, as you have so rightly observed. But get one thing straight here and now. I hold a foreign-going Master's certificate and I have been appointed to command this vessel. From now on, you and you,' she pointed to each of us in turn, 'and everyone else in this ship will take account of that alone and forget my sex.' Her small, well-formed breasts heaving with emotion beneath her tight uniform jacket gave little hope of her latter order being complied with.

She had not finished. 'Furthermore, Mister Thomas,' she went on, 'you are a disgrace to your profession and to the ship. Get your hair cut at once and buy a decent uniform. You look more like an impoverished, middle-aged gigolo than a chief officer.'

She then proceeded to wipe the silly grin off my face. 'And as for you, Mister Marsh, you have nothing to smile about. Your hair is also far too long and, incidentally,' she added with the faintest twinkle in her eyes, 'your flies are undone.'

I was a small boy again as I turned my back to zip up.

There was strong talk of resignation when we got back to the gin bottle. Very half-hearted from me, mind. With a wife and three kids to feed, I had little option but to sit tight.

With Roly it was a different story. 'I'll not take orders from any flaming woman!' he ranted, stalking up and down the confines of my cabin. 'And what's more,' he paused in mid-stride and gestured upwards, 'that bra-burning girl guide up there isn't going to tell me when to get my hair cut. Middle-aged gigolo, indeed!' Roly's vanity had been cut to the quick. He slumped down in my armchair. 'I'll pack my bags and be down that gangway before breakfast in the morning,' he declared firmly.

He was still on board when we sailed forty-eight hours later. Moreover, his hair had been trimmed and his uniform showed signs of a quick visit to the dry cleaners. I concluded —wrongly as it turned out—that he had resigned himself to the inevitable.

He made his first move as we were crossing the Bay of Biscay. A fight, which I later discovered he had stage-managed, broke out on deck between two firemen. Big Somali boys from Tiger Bay, they were. By the time I came shooting out of the engineroom, they were at it hammer and tongs. To my surprise, Roly was standing well back with his arms folded.

'I've sent for the Old Man,' he told me without the trace of a smile on his face.

What happened next rocked both of us back on our heels. The slim figure of Captain Honeywell, immaculately turned out and trailing an aura of lavender water, stepped smartly past us, kneed both fighting men in the groin and moved daintily aside as they collapsed to the deck groaning.

'Bring those men to my cabin at nine o'clock in the morning, Mister Thomas,' she flung at an open-mouthed Roly as she left the deck. I noticed she hadn't as much as laddered her tights in the skirmish.

That little fiasco cost Roly severe loss of face and a fiver each for the firemen concerned.

He sulked for a day or two, then tried a more subtle approach. He began to fuss over Captain Honeywell like a doting admirer. At every possible opportunity he inquired after her comfort, called her "madam" incessantly, rushed to hold her chair when she entered the dining saloon and generally did everything to make her aware of her frail femininity. For a while, she accepted his pampering without a murmur, almost as though she were enjoying it. Then, one evening at dinner, when Roly was being particularly obsequious, she burst out, 'Stop making a damn fool of yourself, Mister Thomas! And—for God's sake—stop calling me madam. Where I come from, that word has quite another connotation.' Roly was forced to retire.

But he was far from beaten. Several evenings later, when we were discussing his lack of progress, he came up with an idea which involved my co-operation. 'She has a bath at seven o'clock every morning,' he told me in a conspiratorial whisper. 'I can hear the water running from the bridge.'

'So?' I asked, wondering how the Captain's bathing habits concerned me.

'It's simple,' he replied eagerly. 'All you have to do is shut off the hot water in the engineroom when I give you the signal from the bridge.' He winked broadly. 'You know how fussy women are. A couple of weeks without a hot bath and she'll be screaming to get off this ship.'

Somehow I couldn't see Captain Honeywell being anything other than flaming mad, but I decided to play along with Roly just for old times' sake.

It was the worst thing I could have done. Captain Honeywell stuck the mysterious lack of hot water for two days without complaint. On the third day I was on the carpet in her office. She stood there, pink-cheeked, buried in her fluffy bathrobe and gave me the biggest dressing down I've ever had. She told me in no uncertain terms that, if I couldn't manage a simple thing like a constant supply of hot water, she would be looking for a new chief engineer at the end of the voyage. Well . . . what could I do?

As it turned out, I left the ship sooner than either of us anticipated. Going into Dakar, a steam pipe burst on the auxiliary boiler and I got the lot in the chest. I was in hospital for three weeks before they flew me home for skin grafts.

I didn't go back to the *Welsh Princess* and I completely lost touch with Roly, although I did hear through the galley wireless that he had finally got his command some months later. Of Captain Honeywell, no word. She seemed to have completely disappeared from the maritime scene.

★   ★   ★   ★

Two more years passed before I finally caught up with Roly again, in of all places, the side bar of *Dirty Marie's* in Casablanca.

'Gin and tonic, Bill?' were his only words of greeting.

'Is there any other drink?' I replied easily, taking his outstretched hand. 'Congratulations, Captain Thomas. You made it to the top at last.'

'Can't keep a good man down for ever, boyo,' he grinned.

I had taken the edge off my thirst before I brought up the subject of Captain Honeywell. 'You got rid of her, then,' I said, signalling for another round. 'What magic did you use?'

He waited for the drinks to arrive before answering. 'No magic, Bill. Married her I did, see. Got a kid now and another one on the way.' He sighed heavily. 'There's one snag, though. Costs me a fortune in shoes does my Frances. She refuses point blank to go barefoot.'

THE LIGHT THAT KILLED

It was one of those rare December nights when the St. George's Channel lowers its jagged horns and lies down like a lamb. A broad ridge of high pressure, reaching down from the frozen plains of Siberia lay dormant across the Western Approaches. Far out in the Atlantic, the raging depressions howled to the moon but here, in the sea of Celtic legends, the night was still. Overhead, a myriad stars winked ice-blue out of a deep velvet sky. There was no trace of fog on a horizon that stretched out to dark infinity.

The *Grey Goose* effortlessly knifed her way through the oily calm at twenty knots plus. Liverpool was 200 miles astern; a fading memory of cosy pubs, cheerful steak bars and Siân, a girl as lovely and as gentle as her lilting name. As I paced the wing of the bridge, filling my lungs with air as cold and pure as a mountain stream, I concluded that life at sea was not without its compensations. Then somebody pulled the plug.

The lights went first. A nervous flicker, followed by complete darkness. Then the steady thump of the *Grey Goose's* 81,000 horsepower diesels faltered and died. Silence joined the darkness. It was so quiet I could hear the engineers cursing five decks below me.

I felt my way back into the wheelhouse and slipped the automatic pilot out of gear. The *Goose* fell off course and, within minutes, she was drifting dead in the water. Thirty-four thousand tons of sophisticated, computerised container ship as helpless as a dumb barge without its tug. I gave a small sigh of relief as the emergency generator came on circuit and dim, orange lights brought a comforting glow back to the wheelhouse. At the same time, the VHF telephone resumed its interrupted chatter on Channel 16. At least, all was normal in the outside world.

Retracing my steps to the wing of the bridge, I stood watching a warning pencil of light sweep regularly across the 15

50

miles of dark water separating the ship from the land. Perched high on the rugged cliffs of Wales, Strumble Head lighthouse was keeping its nightly vigil.

Footsteps rang on the steel ladder leading up from the deck below. The stocky figure of Captain John Fisher came into view. 'Everything all right up here, Third Mate?' he asked.

'No problems, sir,' I replied, turning to meet him.

The Old Man, his pipe filling the darkness with clouds of aromatic smoke, joined me on the compass platform. 'Bloody engineers fluffed it again,' he grumbled in his rich Cornish brogue. 'Water in the fuel this time. The Chief says it won't take more than an hour.' He glanced towards the hidden land. 'How's our position?'

'We'll be all right, sir. The tide's setting off the coast,' I said with all the confidence four years at sea and a brand-new 2nd Mate's ticket can bring.

I sensed a smile. 'Well done, lad.' He nodded in the direction of the flashing light. 'Strumble Head over there, is it?'

'Yes, sir. I picked it up at twenty-five miles. It's a very good light.'

'Aye . . . it is that.' He took a long, ruminative pull at his pipe. 'I could tell you a tale about Strumble Head, you know.'

'Oh . . .,' I said politely. Captain Fisher was coming up to retirement and subject to the odd reminiscence.

He nodded his head slowly. 'It happened a long time ago, mind. Before you were born, lad. Three hundred and fifty lives went that night. And that bloody light killed every one of them.'

I waited for him to go on but, after a moment's silence, he simply squared his shoulders and said briskly, 'All water under the bridge, now.'

I couldn't let it go at that. 'The light killed them?' I asked. 'How?'

Reluctantly, he continued. 'Yes . . . it was wartime, mind. Just another cock-up, I suppose. The last war was full of them —mostly on our side, too. The rotten thing about this one was that it cost us a hospital ship and all those lives.'

The light flashed across us and he fell silent. Remembering.

'What was the ship's name, sir?' I prompted, my curiosity thoroughly aroused.

'Hmm? Oh . . . the *Coromandel Star.* She was on her way back from the Far East with a full load of wounded. Lost her way when she was trying for a landfall on the Welsh coast. There was no radar or satellite navigator in those days, you know.'

As he took a turn up and down the wing, I pondered on the difficulties of navigation without electronic aids. An unreal nightmare for my generation.

'It wouldn't have mattered,' he said, coming to a halt alongside me, 'but when the *Coromandel* was approaching Strumble Head, some stupid bastard ashore decided to switch on the light to give her a fix. I suppose he thought he was doing the right thing but he forgot about the U-boats. There was one lying in wait for just that chance. The *Coromandel* was caught in the beam of the light and took two torpedoes in the engineroom.'

I was shocked, 'They torpedoed a hospital ship?'

He gave a cynical grunt. 'Lad . . . at that stage of the war they torpedoed anything that moved. The *Coromandel Star* wasn't showing lights so, in a way, she was fair game, really. But, at the time, it just seemed bloody inhuman to me. I know we all had to take our chances in those days, but there were women in that ship. Nurses. What harm had they ever done to anyone?' He pocketed his pipe, fished out a large white handkerchief and blew his nose hard.

I had the feeling I was being drawn into one of the dark, personal recesses of his life. I wanted to pull back, yet I couldn't. 'You were in the *Coromandel Star*, sir?' I asked.

He shook his head. 'No. I was 3rd Mate in the old *Ocean Victory.* We were less than twenty miles astern of the *Coromandel* when she bought it. We heard the distress call and went up to full speed—such as it was—but by the time we got up to the position, there was nothing left. No wreckage, no bodies. Just a big patch of dirty oil. She must have gone down in minutes.

Again, time stood still as he scanned the horizon. I broke the silence. 'There were no survivors?'

'Not a single one,' he answered bitterly. 'We searched all night and half the next day. A couple of destroyers came along and gave us a hand after a while, but we didn't find as much as an empty lifejacket between us.'

The rough emotion in his voice urged me to probe deeper. There was a personal involvement here. Perhaps a brother, a near-relative or a close friend had gone down with the ship. 'There was someone . . . someone close to you lost?' I said.

He worried at his eyebrows with the flat of his hand. When he spoke, his voice was low-pitched. 'My fiancée. She was a nurse in the *Coromandel*. We had the wedding fixed for the day after we docked in Liverpool.'

There was a lump in my throat the size of an apple. 'I'm sorry, sir,' I said lamely.

'Nothing for you to be sorry about, lad,' he grunted. 'It wasn't your war.' He had his pipe going again and he puffed away thoughtfully for a few moments. 'In any case, ' he went on, 'I wasn't really the marrying type and we'd only known each other a few weeks. Met out in India. We were both very young—too young, really.' He shrugged. 'Who knows . . . perhaps old Strumble Head over there did me a good turn.' It was brave talk but, as the beam of the lighthouse swept across the bridge, I caught the glisten of tears on Captain Fisher's cheeks.

He turned away quickly and made for the ladder. 'I'm going below,' he said gruffly. 'Call me if you get any trouble.'

The temptation to ask the question proved irresistible. 'When was the *Coromandel Star* sunk, sir?' I called after him.

He stopped with his foot on the top rung of the ladder and looked around. 'December 20th 1943. That's one date I'll never forget.'

I wandered back into the dimly lit wheelhouse, my eyes drawn to the calendar on the bulkhead. December 20th. Forty years ago to the day. I shivered.

'Cup of cocoa, Third?' The standby helmsman, an apparition in dufflecoat, thick scarf and woolly hat, was nudging my arm.

I accepted the steaming mug gratefully. 'Thanks, Jimmy.'

'All part of the service on this watch.' He blew into his hands and stamped his feet, at the same time eyeing me expectantly.

I got the message. Much as I would have been glad of his company, there was no sense in both of us suffering the brass monkey treatment. 'All right. Go and sit in the messroom,' I told him. 'But, if I call, I want you up here at the double. Right?'

When I was once more alone, I leaned back against the radar console, sipping the hot, sweet cocoa, one ear idly tuned to the VHF. The trawlermen were cluttering up Channel 16 as usual. Ribald comments on fish, pubs and women criss-crossed the air waves in a variety of accents. Gradually, my thoughts slipped back to Liverpool, bringing on a warm glow not wholly attributable to the hot drink in my hand. Admittedly, Siân had shot great holes in my bank balance, but what was money for, anyway? To be honest, I had done no more than match generosity with generosity. She had no ulterior motives. There had been no talk of marriage. No shy holding back. When the time was right, she had kissed me and said softly, 'My place?' Sex to Siân was as simple as that. If you wanted it, you had it and put your whole heart and body into it. Which was all very well, I thought with a sudden frown, but who was sharing her warm, inviting bed on this particular frigid December night.

The cheerful background voice of the VHF was suddenly stilled. Puzzled, I reached forward and switched up and down the channels. Nothing. Only the faint, ghostly crackle of far-off atmospherics.

The quiet that followed was unnatural, almost eerie. Without the steady hum of her generators, every creak and rustle of the idling ship became the mournful whimper of a creature in torment. It was then I sensed I was no longer alone on the bridge. With the hairs on the back of my neck beginning to rise, I spun around, spilling hot cocoa over the sleeve of my anorak. Half hidden in the shadows, a woman stood watching; silent.

After a few years at sea, you learn not to panic easily, but the sudden appearance of the bridge of this unknown woman sent a chill racing down my spine. On this voyage, the *Grey Goose* carried no women. No wives, no touchy, feminist cadets. I stood paralysed while my cold-retarded brain groped for an explanation. Then, with a rush, enlightenment dawned. The 2nd Mate's wife, so I had been told, had decided to join the ship only half an hour before sailing from Liverpool. We had not yet met.

I let out a sigh of relief and immediately followed up by giving vent to my feelings. 'For Christ's sake!' I said sharply. 'Do you think that was funny?'

She took a small step back. 'I'm sorry. I didn't mean to startle you,' she said. Her voice was low and husky.

'That's all right,' I grunted, regretting my uncouthness.

Cautiously, she moved out into the light. She was early twenties, tall and with a pleasant, open face, just short of beautiful. She wore a thin robe which did little to hide the gentle swelling of her slim figure. Her short, dark hair was gleaming wet. Just out of the shower, I assumed. The bridge, on a freezing night like this, was the last place she should be. Another thought occurred to me and my built-in alarm bell gave a warning ping. It was eleven o'clock at night and her husband, who had the middle watch, would be fast asleep in his bunk. Yet, here she was, naked under that robe I was prepared to guarantee, calmly hanging about the bridge. There could be only two explanations for her presence. Either she was in trouble—and the serene expression on her face belied that—or she had an ulterior motive. Wives who play the extramarital game while on board ship are not unknown.

She smiled and came towards me, her hand outstretched. 'I'm Diana,' she said simply.

Reluctantly, I took her hand. It was ice-cold. 'Tim Walker, 3rd Mate.'

She nodded, then gave a tinkling laugh. 'I'm not a bit like that, Tim.'

I let go of her hand. 'Like what?'

She put her head on one side. 'You were thinking . . .'

The alarm bells in my head rang loudly. She was either very practised at this sort of thing or she was able to read my thoughts. 'Sorry I was rude,' I mumbled, 'but you did give me a fright.' I eyed her flimsy robe and gave an involuntary shiver. 'Don't you think you ought to put some clothes on? You'll catch your death up here.'

She laughed again. 'That's impossible.'

I shrugged. She was a strange girl all right. And, for some reason, she brought out the long-dormant gentleman in me. I peeled off my anorak and draped it over her shoulders. 'Your need is greater than mine,' I said lamely.

She looked up at me and shook her head. 'It's not really. But thank you for the thought.' Then she snuggled down into the warm coat like a cat finding a new home.

We were very close, my hands still on her shoulders, our bodies almost touching. Her perfume was light, muted, as old-fashioned as English Lavendar. I looked down into the deep brown of her eyes, feeling the pull of an irresistible tide. Then, her generous mouth softened into a sad smile and she gave a small shake of her head. The warning was unmistakeable.

I backed off hastily. I had been on the point of making a pass at the wife of a fellow officer—an unpardonable sin in any seaman's book. And she had obviously read my mind. This was not only dangerous, it was uncanny. I turned to move away from her but she caught my arm in a firm grip. 'The light!' she cried in a strangled voice. I followed her terrified gaze. It was fixed on the regular flash of the lighthouse sweeping across the horizon.

I was baffled by her sudden fear. 'It's only Strumble Head,' I said reassuringly,

Her face was drawn, masklike. 'Why is it on?' she asked in a small, frightened voice.

Good question, but it didn't fit. This girl was scared, really scared. 'It usually comes on at night,' I said roughly, hoping to turn her away from hysteria.

It worked. Her shoulders drooped and she turned away from the light. 'Of course,' she whispered. 'Silly of me.' When she looked up at me again, her smile was back. 'Tell me about John Fisher,' she asked. 'Is he a good captain?'

This was a new tack. It was also a perfectly reasonable question for a newly-joined wife to ask. A good captain could turn her voyage into an idyllic ocean cruise. A bad one could make it hell. 'Captain Fisher's one of the best,' I answered truthfully.

'Did he ever marry?'

I bristled. What did the Old Man's private life have to do with this woman? 'Look, Mrs. . . . er . . . Diana,' I said irritably, 'it's none of your . . .' I broke off. I was locked into her eyes again, being drawn out of my depth by that strange, overwhelming force. 'No. He was never married,' I heard myself answering dully.

She continued probing. 'Was there never anyone?'

I was determined to stay silent, yet I was unable to do so. 'There was a girl, once. She died in the war.' The story of the torpedoed hospital ship was still fresh in my mind.

'No other woman since then?'

The cold of the night suddenly bit into my bones and I shuddered. 'I don't . . . I don't think so,' I answered hesitantly.

Her lips parted and a sparkle came into her eyes. 'Just one more question, Tim. Is John Fisher happy?'

I nodded silently and, as I did, the wheelhouse was filled with a warmth that spoke of reassurance and peace. Smiling, the girl reached up and kissed me on the cheek. 'Thank you, Tim,' she whispered. Then, she slipped out of my coat and disappeared back into the shadows from which she had come.

'Diana!' I called, but there was no answer. Retrieving my coat from the deck where she had let it fall, I wormed my way back into its fur-lined haven, wondering whether she had been real or just part of some muddled dream brought on by the magic of the night. I had no time to pursue my thoughts for, at that moment, the long-silent VHF came back to life with a burst of inane but comforting small-talk. Seconds later, lights and instruments began to flick on in quick succession. The radar screen flared and resumed its monotonous sweep, while the gyro compass gave out a healthy clicking sound as it realigned. Before I could reach the telephone, the engines coughed and began to take up a slow, rhythmic beat. The *Grey Goose* was once more alive and under way.

Captain Fisher arrived on the bridge as I was hastily pencilling in a position on the chart. 'Drifted much, has she?' he asked, leaning over my shoulder.

'Hardly moved an inch, sir,' I answered without straightening up.

He gave a satisfied grunt. 'Neap tides. Just as well, too.'

I followed him out onto the wing of the bridge, where we stood quietly watching the white water cream away from the bows as the ship gathered speed. 'Nice night,' he continued, sniffing at the clear air.

'Perfect, sir. Christmas weather.'

He snorted. 'Don't talk to me about Christmas. That 2nd Mate's wife's been pounding my ear on the subject for the past hour. She seems to think I was personally responsible for sailing the ship before Christmas. An outspoken lady is young Susan. Haven't met her, have you?'

'Susan?' My mind was reeling, 'You say she's been with you for the past hour?'

He gave me a queer look. 'That's right. A dab hand at Scrabble, she is. Beat the pants off the Purser and me.'

I was frightened but I had to know the truth. 'What does she look like? The 2nd Mate's wife.'

He must have thought I was unhinged, but he answered, 'Oh . . . blonde. Short . . . about five foot three, I'd say. Nice little figure but a bit heavy on top, if you know what I mean.'

The blood in my vein ran ice-cold. Had I imagined the caress of her voice, the cool touch of her lips, the soft fragrance of her perfume? I sought out the light of Strumble Head, now near to dipping below the horizon, and the answer was there. I turned to the man at my side. 'Sir. The girl on the hospital ship . . . your fiancée. What was her name?'

He answered without hesitation. 'Diana. Why?'

I shook my head and looked astern to where the phosphorescent wake of the *Grey Goose* stretched back forty years.

CHRISTMAS ROGUE

Captain Richard Holmes straightened up from his study of the radar screen. 'God rest ye merry gentlemen . . .,' he sang in a low, off-key. Holmes was well pleased with his lot and had every reason to be so. The English Channel was on its best behaviour. Fine, crystal clear weather, with just a few whitecaps. Enough wind to keep the fog away but not enough to mar the ship's excellent progress. Another six hours would see the *Gulf Heron* off the pilot station at Folkestone then, given the blessing of a co-operative pilot, she would be safely moored at Thameshaven in time for breakfast on Christmas Day. A programme founded on supposition but well within the capability of a man willing to take a risk or two.

The rest would be up to the local Maritime Mafia, as Holmes was in the habit of calling the small army of Customs, Immigration and Port Health officials who would board on arrival. Being the festive season, it was to be hoped these guardians of the law would be in a benevolent mood. In any case, the odd bottle of Black Label—Company's expense, of course—would be bound to speed up the formalities. Holmes was in no doubt that he could be off the ship and making tracks for home by midday. Transport presented no problem. The battered old Rover, with his wife, Martha, at the wheel, would be on the quay waiting, as they had waited on so many quays over so many years.

Yes, Holmes concluded warmly, Christmas with the family would be a fitting end to a long and successful voyage. Five thousand miles across the Atlantic perched on top of 50,000 tons of highly volatile jet fuel entitled a man to such a reward.

Not that it had been an unduly difficult voyage. The usual running battle with that cantankerous, old reprobate of a chief engineer; engine revolutions always too low and fuel consumption too high. And, as must be expected, the weather alternating between force 10 and flat calm accompanied by dense fog. The Atlantic had only two faces, both of them ugly. But, ageing though she might be, the ship had stood up to it all without a murmur. No cause for complaint there.

In her younger days, the *Gulf Heron*, 30,327 tons gross, had been regarded as the ultimate of her breed, matched in size and equipage only by the big passenger vessels of that era. Those who sailed in her considered themselves to be members of a rather exclusive club. Overnight, with the spawning of the 350,000 ton supertankers, *Gulf Heron* had been relegated to the ranks of the insignificant—a mere tiddler in a sea populated by whales. From then on, a certain amount of degeneration had inevitably set in. She now wore the air of a no longer young matron; trim and tight-waisted still, but fighting a losing battle against the ravages of time. Despite her shortcomings, she was still capable of a comfortable 16 knots. At this speed she now progressed up the English Channel, nudged and prodded onwards by a complement of officers and men determined to see Christmas on their native soil.

Holmes moved away from the radar, satisfied with the picture presented. The broken outline of the land matched up with the winking lights of the Isle of Wight, which loomed darkly on the port side. There were a few ship echoes on the screen but all seemed to be passing well clear of the *Heron*. Holmes zipped closed his padded anorak and took station in the wing of the bridge, breathing deep of the cold, clean air. A small fishing boat, working lights incandescent in the darkness, drifted slowly past the beam. From fine to port came the brilliant flash of the Greenwich Buoy, the forty-foot, computer-controlled floating lighthouse marking the commencement of the Dover Strait traffic separation scheme.

Now comes the difficult bit, Holmes thought wryly, and not without a twinge of anxiety. Ahead lay one hundred miles of shoal water with the highest density of traffic in the world. To be sure, the rules governing the conduct of ships in this narrow through-waterway were strict but there were bound to be some rogues abroad on a fine night like this. They—and he was quite clear in his mind as to who *they* were—regarded traffic separation lanes as conveniences for use in thick weather only. Clear weather offered the opportunity to cut corners providing, of course, it was dark and no one was able to point the accusing finger.

Casting his thoughts back, Holmes remembered a fine evening when he was rounding Ushant, not many summers ago. The weather had been perfect with a horizon so sharp that he had not felt it necessary to search ahead with the radar. Then the other ship had appeared out of the dusk without warning, steaming in the wrong lane, navigation lights unlit. Even with the helm jammed hard over and engines racing full astern, it had been a very near miss. It just went to show how easily you could get caught if you once dropped your guard. He had been carrying a full load of jet fuel on that voyage, too. It could have been a very messy accident.

Holmes paused in his reminiscing to wipe away the beads of cold sweat forming on his forehead. It was strange how the mind would never let go of experiences like that. They kept coming back for replay like old 78's passed down from the attic.

'We seem to have lost the Greenwich Buoy, sir.' The 3rd Officer had materialised soundlessly in the bridge wing.

Holmes was jerked rudely out of his thoughts. 'Lost the buoy? What do you mean, *lost it?* You don't just *lose* buoys, lad!' he said irritably.

Even as he spoke, Holmes realised what the young officer was trying to communicate to him. He searched the horizon ahead and drew a complete blank. The flashing light of the Greenwich Buoy and the bright stern lights of the two ships which had overtaken the *Heron* in the past hour had disappeared from sight. The once easily recognisable line between sea and sky had become indistinct. A quick check on the radar confirmed his worst fears. There was fog close ahead.

Without leaving the radar, he called over his shoulder. 'Phone the engineroom! Warn them we're running into fog. I want the controls manned all the time.' He paused and debated silently. This could ruin the whole carefully laid plan. Reduce speed now and his would be the empty chair at the family table tomorrow. Christmas for the whole crew of the *Gulf Heron* would be just another near miss. He jerked erect, his decision made. 'And tell the engineers that, under no circumstances are they to reduce speed unless I give the word,' he added firmly.

★   ★   ★   ★

The motor vessel *Spiros K*, 7200 tons of rust-pitted plates, sagging under a full cargo of steel scrap, slid heavily through the flat winter calm of the English Channel. Below the waterline, her ancient engine, pushed to maximum revolutions, hammered out a furious and incessant tattoo.

On the bridge, Captain Georgios Andreados paced the starboard wing impatiently; that is to say he waddled five paces forward and five paces back. The bridge wing was small and Captain Andreados was running to fat. He was not normally a vain man but the fact that he was fast acquiring a pot-belly worried him. When a man is married to a woman twenty-five years his junior, the retention of a youthful image assumes a niggling priority.

But this particular problem was not uppermost in the mind of Andreados on this bitterly cold Christmas Eve. His mind was firmly locked on to the necessity of an early docking in Cherbourg on the following morning. From that port, where the *Spiros K* was to make a brief stop for bunkers, Andreados, after eighteen long, weary months on board was to hand over his command and proceed on leave. An early docking was imperative, for the only Athens bound plane of the day left Cherbourg at 0930. If Andreados was to be sure of enjoying the luxury of Christmas with his young bride, he had to be on that plane. It was for this reason he was prepared to break every rule in the book.

Outward bound from Antwerp, the *Spiros K*'s prudent and, indeed mandatory, route through the Straits of Dover lay close to the Kentish coast, passing in sight of Dover, Dungeness and Beachy Head. Only when abeam of Newhaven and clear of the traffic separation lanes, was she free to cut across Channel and assume a south-westerly course for Cherbourg. But Captain Andreados was having none of this bureaucratic nonsense. In his mind, the law was the servant of the individual, to be bent and moulded to fit the circumstances prevailing. Taking the more northerly, and proper, route meant a longer passage and, consequently, a later arrival at Cherbourg. His cherished dream of Christmas at home would be shattered. The solution, however illegal and fraught with danger, had been quite clear from the start.

During the daylight hours, Andreados had kept meticulously to his lawfully allotted side of the traffic separations schemes. With the coming of darkness, he had slipped across into the north-east-going lane, weaving in and out of the path of on-coming ships like a lone jogger caught on the wrong pavement during the rush hour. With the VHF radio switched off and the radar unserviceable—the normal state of readiness of the cranky old set—Andreados reasoned that, by rendering himself deaf and half-blind, he would be less conspicuous. So far, it had worked. At times, he had been close, very close, to on-coming ships but he had not been challenged. That the Dover Coastguard already had him under radar surveillance caused him little concern. There would be no positive identification. On a black night such as this, the *Spiros K* was just another bow wave.

Breaking off from his contemplation of past events, Andreados sniffed at the cold night air. He frowned and sniffed again. The increased humidity was unmistakeable. Cursing aloud, he thumped the bridge rail with his clenched fist. He, of all people, should have known there was no way through these wretched waters without being beset by fog.

He stamped into the wheelhouse, kicking savagely at the defunct radar as he passed. 'Nico!' he bawled.

'Here, Uncle!' a startled voice answered from the shadows. Nicholaos Pateris, 3rd Officer of the *Spiros K* and reputed son of Captain Andreados' first wife's brother, had been deep in his habitual erotic fantasy. By pure chance, this featured a young lady bearing an uncanny resemblance to the second Mrs. Andreados.

'Wake up, you son of a back-street whore!' Andreados roared. 'There is fog coming. Post a lookout in the bows at once. Stupid boy!'

★   ★   ★   ★

The duty operator of the Dover Coastguard radar surveillance station tipped back his chair and regarded the radar screen with satisfaction. As was fitting for this Christmas Eve, the Strait was quiet. Between the outlines of the English and French coasts, brightly etched on the screen, only a few ship echoes moved. Even the ferries seemed to have stilled their frantic criss-crossing of the traffic lanes.

'If you ask me, Mog, most of our brave sailormen are snugged down for the night in the nearest pub. It's a soft life at sea these days all right.' The operator's remarks were addressed to his sole companion, a sleek, over-fed cat occupying the top of a filing cabinet. The animal peered back through slitted eyes but offered no comment.

Stifling a yawn, the operator glanced at his watch. It was coming up to 2145. Fifteen more minutes, providing no one hit the panic button, and he was off watch, the rest of the night his. He debated joining the party, already well established in the canteen below him. The muffled sounds of music and laughter drifting up to the tower were a sore temptation. He decided against. Eighteen years at sea and every Christmas spent afloat or in some god-forsaken port drinking himself stupid to kill the loneliness—enough was enough. Tonight was for hot toddies in front of a crackling log fire, presents under the Christmas tree, the excited whispering of the children in bed . . .

Reluctantly, his eyes wandered back to the glowing radar screen. Moments passed before he became aware of the change taking place in the normal pattern. Close southwards of the stationary blip marking the Bassurelle light-vessel, a small echo was inching its way slowly to the west against the customary flow of traffic. The operator's chair slammed upright and he was instantly alert. He had a rogue; a ship violating the rules of the traffic separation scheme. He groaned aloud. A rogue at this stage of the watch was the last thing he needed. And this one looked like being a real beauty: heading west in the north-east lane, hell-bent on destruction. It was goodbye to hot toddies by the fire. He would have to stay with this one until she cleared the separation lanes. With a shrug of resignation, he unclipped the handset of the VHF. 'All ships! All ships! This is Dover Strait Coastguard. One vessel in the north-east lane, position 195 degrees, 2.2 miles from the Bassurelle light-vessel. Course 245 degrees, speed approximately 12 knots. This course does not comply with the regulations. I say again . . .'

★   ★   ★   ★

The *Spiros K* was in dense fog. The loom of her foremast light, a scant 250 feet forward of her bridge had long since been swallowed by the murk. Wrapping close around her, the white, amorphous blanket created an eerie silence, broken only by the echoing thump of the ship's engines. She had not reduced speed, neither was she sounding her whistle, as prescribed by the rules governing the conduct of vessels in fog. Her blunt blows, backed by 12,000 tons of ship and cargo, pushed relentlessly on through the opaque darkness.

Captain Andreados was working on the shaky hypothesis that all ships in his immediate vicinity would be equipped with radar, that they would be using the same to full advantage and would, therefore, keep out of his way. That his actions were those of a madman did not occur to him. He was obsessed with the necessity of a quick passage to Cherbourg. For the time being, luck appeared to be on his side. On more than one occasion he had detected the muffled beat of a ship's engine close by; once the frenzied howl of a siren and distant cries of alarm borne on the still night air but Andreados kept his ears shut tight. A few short miles and he would be clear of the traffic lanes.

Hitching his belt up over his developing paunch, Captain Andreados hunched forward across the bridge rail, willing his eyes to penetrate the blank wall of fog confronting him. His sharpened hearing caught the plaintive moan of a distant foghorn. Was it another ship; another wanderer in the murk? He jerked his head erect and listened attentively, one ear cocked. His fingers beat time on the rail as he counted out the passing seconds. The blast came again, bringing a smile of relief to his face. Exactly thirty seconds between blasts. The Greenwich Buoy was somewhere out there to starboard. Almost jaunty now, Andreados resumed his perambulation of the bridge wing. His attention thus relaxed, he failed to hear another faint, but more urgent blast ahead.

★   ★   ★   ★

Captain Holmes was also navigating by the Greenwich Buoy but, unlike Andreados, his contact was a precise and definite one. The strong signals thrown back by the radar reflector and the responder beacon on the buoy could not be mistaken.

Holmes took another turn up and down the wheelhouse. He was on course with no other ships threatening his progress, yet he was unable to subdue the feeling that, in pressing on at full speed, he was taking an unjustifiable risk. How many times, he reflected guiltily, had he hammered into his junior officers the theory that poor visibility must be countered by moderate speed? If things went wrong on this night, the court of inquiry would crucify him.

The fog, now more dense than ever, seemed to be filtering its way into the wheelhouse. This may just have been the effect of the condensing breaths of the occupants of the confined space but it did nothing to allay Holmes' increasing anxiety. He rubbed his reddened eyes and stoically regarded the weather. It was as thick as a hedge; the visibility down to less than fifty yards.

Common sense told him to take the way off the ship there and then; to drop down to a crawl and feel his way up the Channel as any prudent seaman would. But, he argued silently and convincingly, what was the point in carrying radar and Decca navigator if he was not prepared to make full use of them? The *Gulf Heron*'s position was being constantly and accurately fixed and, at all times, he was able to monitor and plot the actions of any ships in the vicinity. He made up his mind firmly. He was damned if he was going to miss that Christmas dinner. The disappointment he would suffer personally was of no great moment. It was the others in the family, his wife, Martha, young Jane back from Australia with her brood of kids, Martin who, with his brand-new wife had travelled from God-knows-where in India—not to mention old Uncle George. He just couldn't let them down.

The voice of the 3rd Officer cut into his thoughts. 'Ship fine to port, sir! Six miles off and closing.'

Holmes crossed swiftly to the radar and peered over the young officer's shoulder. The implications of the plot were ominous. The other vessel was coming down on the opposite course and obviously in the wrong lane. They would pass port to port but close; very close. He cursed roundly. This was the Christmas Rogue he had dreaded. There was a tremor of unease in his voice as he gave his orders. 'Five degrees to starboard! Start sounding the whistle.'

The deafening blare of the *Gulf Heron*'s powerful air whistle filled the wheelhouse and boomed out into the fog.

★   ★   ★   ★

The lookout man crouched in the bows of the *Spiros K*, lulled into half-sleep by the gentle swish of the bow wave, was brought scrambling to his feet by the trumpeting roar bursting on his eardrums. Long, long ago, in his native Africa, he had heard such a sound; the roar of a maddened charging bull elephant. Sobbing with fear, the man ran headlong down the deck, pursued by all the demons of Hell.

Georgios Andreados did not fear the horrendous sound— he knew well what it was—but he was mortally afraid of the decision he now had to make. The awesome warning, echoed and refracted by the fog, seemed to come from all sides. He had only seconds in which to act. But which way should he run? Holy Mother! Which way?

Another blast sounded; fainter this time. But there was no doubt the source was to starboard of the *Spiros K*. Yes, Andre-

ados decided, the danger lay to starboard. 'Hard-a-port!' he
yelled. 'Hard-a-port!'

As the automatic timer of the Greenwich Buoy, hidden
and forgotten to starboard, clicked off the seconds to the next
blast of its fog signal, the deep-laden hull of the *Spiros K*
swung ponderously to port, into the path of the *Gulf Heron*.
The dice were thrown, the game lost.

For those on the bridge of the tanker, the first, and only
sight of the impending disaster was the blunt bow of the
Spiros K breaking through the fog like a gigantic battering
ram propelled by unseen hands. With a screech of rending
metal, it struck the *Heron* amidships. Showers of sparks
fanned out to meet the great gush of fuel and gas spurting
from the ruptured cargo tanks.

Men keeping watch in ships twenty miles away gasped in
horror as the surrounding fog flashed blood red. A sonorous
thunderclap rolled seventy miles up Channel and rattled
angrily at the windows of the Dover Coastguard watch
tower.

The improvised choir in the canteen sang on uninter-
rupted, 'God rest ye merry gentlemen . . .'

THE RETURN OF THE FRENCH

'Pint of bitter, Gladys,' I said, leaning on the bar and soaking up a small river of slops with the sleeve of my best blue blazer.

Gladys John gave a flick of her pinkish blonde hair and stuck out her bosom as she drew my pint. Lovely girl, Gladys, even if she was getting on a bit and could never make up her mind about the colour of her hair. Good at her job, too. The froth reached right to the rim of the glass without a drop of beer spilt. 'No fishing tonight then, Emlyn?' she asked as she handed the glass across.

I took a long swig and wiped the froth off my beard with the back of my hand. 'Gladys, *bach* ... it's Saturday night. A man has to have *some* time off. Besides, it's the twenty-third of February and no one in his right mind goes out into Cardigan Bay tonight.'

She shivered and her face went white under the make-up. 'Don't you even talk about it, Emlyn Owen!' she breathed, reaching for the glass of vodka she kept under the bar.

'No talk,' I said. 'It's getting drunk I am tonight and then home early. You won't catch me outside when the *dead ones* are around.'

The poor girl shivered again, her teeth chattering on the rim of her glass. I felt a bit rotten but, then, the twenty-third of February is no joke in Fishguard.

I put my back to the bar and looked around the room. A very comfortable sight the lounge bar of the Kings Arms was, with its low ceiling supported by genuine oak beams and roaring log fire reflecting in the copper warming pans and horse brasses hanging on the whitewashed walls. All very much as it must have been on that night one hundred and eighty-six years ago.

At the far end of the bar, I could see the landlord, Caradog Jenkins, with his head close to a customer. A stranger too. In Fishguard at this time of the year strangers stand out like scarecrows in a ploughed field. 'Who's that Caradog's talking to?' I asked, turning round to Gladys.

Her glass was empty and the colour back in her cheeks. 'English,' she said with a sniff. 'And pumping Mister Jenkins for all he's worth.'

I looked again. Caradog Jenkins didn't seem to need any pumping. Thumbs hooked in the pockets of his waistcoat, the sweat shining on his bald head, he was talking nineteen to the dozen. The well-dressed stranger—a man in his mid-forties—was listening carefully. My nose twitching, I decided to investigate.

'Evening, Caradog,' I said, making a casual approach, pint in hand. The stranger looked up with a frown. Annoyed at being interrupted by some ignorant Welsh peasant, I suppose.

Caradog gave me a nod. 'You in for the 'Anniversary', Emlyn?'

'Of course I am, boyo. Wouldn't miss it for the world.' I looked around. 'Not many in tonight, though. Taken their custom over to the Anchor, I suppose. New barmaid over there, Caradog. Young piece of stuff. High time you pensioned old Gladys off, you know.' Pulling his leg I was, Gladys John being his wife's cousin.

But the Englishman took me seriously. 'Oh come, now!' he said in a posh voice. 'I've just visited the Anchor Hotel and that barmaid's no great shakes. Your Gladys looks like a very efficient young lady.'

Now, if there's one thing I can't stand it's know-all English tourists trying to tell us Welsh what's what. As far as I was concerned, Gladys was over the hill and no argument. 'You an expert on barmaids then, Mister?' I growled, drawing myself up to my full five feet six inches. It is unfortunate that most of my race are so short-arsed.

Knowing my temper, Caradog was quick to jump in. 'No need to get stroppy, Emlyn. Mister Spencer here is a writer from London. Interested in us, he is. Going to do a book about Fishguard.' He turned to the stranger. 'This is Captain Emlyn Owen, Mister Spencer. He'll have a tale or two to tell you about the waters around here, I'm sure.'

The stranger slipped off the bar stool and held out his hand. Big man he was, with dark hair just greying at the temples. His eyes were smiling but no warmth in them, if you know what I mean. 'How do you do, Captain Owen? I'm George Spencer,' he said, very friendly now that he knew I was a captain. I'm only a trawler skipper really but the people in West Wales have got a thing about sea captains. Put on a peaked cap and buy yourself a rowing boat and it's Captain this and Captain that right away. Mind you, it opens a lot of doors, I can tell you.

I shook his hand, giving him a reluctant, 'Pleased to meet you.'

He pointed to my glass. 'Will you take a drink with me, Captain? What's it to be . . . another pint? Or would you like something short?'

Well, what was I to do? I couldn't very well refuse to take a drink from the man, even if he was English. 'Thank you, Mister Spencer,' I said. 'I'll take a whisky, if you don't mind.'

Spencer took out a pigskin wallet and put a ten pound note on the bar. 'Two large whiskies, Landlord . . . and whatever you fancy yourself.'

Caradog Jenkins nearly had a fit. We don't see ten pound notes too often in Fishguard and the last time anyone ordered double whiskies in the Kings Arms must have been when Lloyd George was made Prime Minister.

I rolled the whisky around on my tongue, liking the clean bite of it. A peculiar lot the Scotch may be but they make a good drop of drink.

When I was looking through the bottom of my empty glass, I said, 'Why a book about Fishguard, Mister Spencer? There's nothing to write about here.'

He signalled Caradog to refill my glass and then leaned towards me. 'What about the invasion of Britain then, Captain? There's a story in that, surely.'

Now that was different. A bit of an expert on the subject of the last invasion of Britain, I am. As everybody knows, it took place in February 1797 at Carreg Wastad, a rocky beach not eight miles along the coast road from where we were sitting. 'You've come to the right place if you want to know about the Invasion,' I told Spencer. 'The French surrendered to Lord Cawdor here in the *Kings Arms*—in this very room.'

'One hundred and eighty-six years ago tonight,' Caradog added in a hushed voice.

'That's double cause for celebration then,' the Englishman said going for his wallet. Caradog and I didn't have the heart to say no. Whiskies all round again, it was.

While Caradog poured, I looked around me to see how the peasants were doing. The place was filling up, with Gladys John pulling pints as fast as her plump arms would work. There was a lot of shouting and laughter. Christmas Eve all over again it was.

Spencer raised his glass, catching the mood. 'Damnation to the French eh, Captain?'

'Very true,' I said. 'It's not often we Welsh get a chance to give the French a good hiding—except at the Arms Park, of course. So February the 23rd is a very special day for us. Call it the 'Anniversary', we do.'

He nodded. 'Yes . . . I had heard about it.' He went quiet for a minute and then came out with a funny question. 'By the way, do you get any regular French visitors over here at this time of the year?'

I was about to let him know we don't let Frogs near the place, summer or winter, when Caradog chipped in. 'Three of them,' he said, wiping down the bar with his cloth. 'Staying at the Bay Hotel down by the harbour. They're there for the last week in February every year, so Gwyn Phillips, the manager, tells me.'

Spencer drained his glass. 'Hmm . . . very interesting, Mister Jenkins,' was all he said.

A good night we had after that, with Spencer buying the drinks and Caradog and me feeding him stories about the Invasion. It was fair exchange, I thought, even if we did embroider the tales a bit. We told him how one thousand and four hundred French soldiers landed at Carreg Wastad on the night of the 23rd February 1797, with the intention of hoisting the tricolour over Pembrokeshire—and the rest of Wales, given half a chance. All that stood between them and the town of

Fishguard was Lord Cawdor and a small detachment of the Fishguard Fencibles—a kind of local Home Guard. They would have stood no chance of stopping the French if the farmhouses around Carreg Wastad hadn't been well stocked with wine which, ironically, had come from a French ship wrecked off the beach a couple of weeks before. Of course, the French troops soon got in amongst this wine and, by the time the sun came up, they were legless.

'A lot of people around here will tell you a different story,' I pointed out to Spencer. 'But you can take my word for it, the only reason the Fencibles won was because the French couldn't stand up, let alone shoot.'

That had Spencer laughing but he shut up quick when Caradog put his cloth over the pumps and called time. 'Good Lord!' he burst out. 'You're not closing already, are you? It's only half past nine.'

Caradog was embarrassed. 'Well . . . you see, Mister Spencer,' he said, dipping his finger in a pool of beer and making circles on the top of the bar, 'this being the 23rd of February, people don't like being out late—especially those who live on the other side of the bay, near to Carreg Wastad.'

'The last bus goes from the Square at ten o'clock,' I put in, thinking it was time to shift if I was going to catch it.

This was like offering bait to a fish. Spencer perked up. 'Do I smell another story here?' he said.

Caradog was red in the face now but, fair dues, he spoke up. 'It's not a very pretty story, Mister Spencer. You know some of it but you don't know about the *dead ones*. It's because of them we close early tonight.'

You could almost see Spencer's ears flapping. 'The *dead ones?*'

Caradog nodded. 'Yes, sir. You see . . . when the French landed that night—the 23rd of February 1797—they got pretty drunk, as Captain Owen has already told you. Well . . . when they heard Lord Cawdor was advancing with the Fishguard Fencibles, some of the French soldiers staggered back down to the beach and took to the boats. No stomach for the fight, I suppose.'

'That lot's never been any different,' I added for good measure. All the whisky I'd downed was beginning to have an effect.

Caradog ignored me and went on. 'When the boats were about half a mile from the shore, a nasty gale blew up and there was a panic. Some of the boats sank and over fifty Frenchmen were drowned, so they say.' He leaned over the bar and lowered his voice. 'Now, every year, on the 23rd of February—this very night—those poor drowned souls come back to haunt Carreg Wastad. Eleven o'clock is their time, Mister Spencer so, if you'll take my advice, you'll be safe indoors by then.'

George Spencer nearly fell off his stool. 'Do you seriously mean to tell me,' he said, 'that because of this ... er ... ghost story, the whole countryside locks itself indoors by eleven o'clock. It's a joke, surely.'

'No joke, Mister Spencer,' I said. 'Nobody out after eleven tonight. Pubs close at half nine, last bus across the bay at ten —and I'll be on it for one.'

He looked at me as though I was daft. 'Now, don't tell me *you* believe all this rubbish, Captain? A man of your calibre ...'

Trying the old soft soap, he was, but I wasn't falling for it. 'Don't take my word for it,' I said. 'Ask old Dai Rees-the-Post. Two years ago tonight, he missed the last bus and was daft enough to walk home. Got as far as Carreg Wastad, when they came at him out of the water. Seaweed in their hair and maggots crawling all over their dead faces, so he said.'

Spencer tried to laugh it off. 'I'd like to meet the old chap. Add a touch of humour to my book, I'm sure.'

'You'll have to go to Haverfordwest, then,' I told him. 'Old Dai's in the mental home there. Off his head, he is.' I emptied my glass. 'Thanks for the drinks, Mister Spencer. Time for me to catch the bus. I live on the other side of Carreg Wastad, same as poor Dai Rees did.'

He grabbed my arm as I stood up to go. 'Oh, come on, Captain!' he said, very friendly. 'Time for another quick one. I tell you what ... I'll give you a lift home in my car. I'm staying over at Trehowel Farm. You'll be perfectly safe with me. Forget the bus.'

I should have known better but, then, I could never resist a free drink.

★   ★   ★   ★

Of course, the one-for-the-road let to two, then three and, by the time we climbed into George Spencer's old Cortina, it was half past ten. I had a good load on and no mistake. It was a long, bumpy ride along the coast road, with the Englishman singing 'Land of Hope and Glory' at the top of his voice and me nearly throwing up every time we went round a corner. To make matters worse, the drink began to wear off and I found myself thinking about those corpses coming ashore at Carreg Wastad. Then, when we were bouncing along the half-made road that runs past the beach, the engine packed up.

Spencer stopped singing and sobered up very quick. He pulled and fiddled with switches, cursing all the time, but the engine wouldn't start. He turned to me. 'You know anything about cars, Captain?'

I shook my head. Being a self-employed fisherman, I do know a bit about engines—there being no garages out in Cardigan Bay. But not even the Queen of England was going to get me out of that car.

The lights had gone when the engine stopped so we sat there in the pitch darkness, with me keeping my head down in case I saw something terrible outside. We were right opposite where the French had landed and I was feeling very uncomfortable indeed. After a minute or two, I said, 'Mister Spencer, it's nearly eleven o'clock and the French will be coming ashore at any minute now. We'd better lock all doors and start praying.' It was not that I was really frightened but, with ghosts, you never know.

Even in the dark, I could see he was giving me a queer look. Then he shrugged and said, 'All right, Captain. You sit tight. I'll get out and take a shufti under the bonnet. You keep an eye on the beach.'

Which was as good as saying, 'You're a bloody coward, Emlyn Owen.' It wasn't true of course. I've been a fisherman all my life and used to riding out the gales of Cardigan Bay in a 32-footer. But this was different. This was the 23rd of February and the French were about.

While Spencer's torch was bobbing about outside, the wind started to moan and I could hear the waves crashing on the beach. Only once did I look down there and I was sorry I did. I'll swear I saw lights on the water; just like the lights of small boats pulling for the shore. I was working up to my first heart attack when Spencer climbed back into the car.

'Well, that's it, Captain,' he said matter of factly. 'Battery's as flat as a pancake. We're in for a long walk, I'm afraid.'

'Not me Mister Spencer,' I said quickly. 'I'm not getting out of this car.'

He sniffed. 'Up to you, Captain.' He said quiet for a minute, then he turned to me. 'Afraid of the *dead ones*, are you?'

'Umm . . .' I was petrified, to tell the truth.

There was a long silence between us and I knew what he was thinking. Suddenly, he sat up. 'What would you say if I told you the ghosts of Carreg Wastad were real, live Frenchmen?'

I kept my head down. 'What do you know about it, Mister Spencer? There's been ghosts here for one hundred and eighty-six years.'

'If you'll come down to the beach with me, I'll prove you wrong.'

I was shaking my head before he finished talking. He must have thought I was in a bad state because he took a flask out of his overcoat pocket and handed it to me without a word. I took a long swig. Ten-year old whisky it was. Like liquid fire. Between us, we emptied the flask, me getting most of it. Then, Spencer handed me a torch and got out of the car. Like a damn fool, I followed him.

The night was as black as a witches den and we hadn't gone more than a few yards before he stopped suddenly and I walked straight into his back. 'Did you hear that?' he asked in a loud whisper.

I could hear the wind sighing, the sea rattling the pebbles on the beach below us and a flaming owl hooting over towards Llanwnda Church. Enough to put the wind up anyone. 'What was it?' I asked, trying to keep the shake out of my voice.

'Voices,' he said. 'Come on, Captain!' Then, he was off, running bent double towards the beach.

He had locked the car when we left so it was no good me going back. I could either stand there in the pitch black shaking like an old woman or go after him. The moon broke through the clouds and something rustled in the gorse bushes behind me so I didn't have to think any more. I made for the beach at the double. At least Spencer was human.

I caught up with him kneeling in the shadow of a big rock, not ten yards from the water. 'There's somebody up there!' I gasped, throwing myself down alongside him.

'I know,' he said, as unconcerned as you like. He was watching the water closely. Suddenly, he grabbed my arm and pointed out to sea. 'Look! Out there!'

I pressed myself back against the rock, wishing I could climb inside it. There was no getting away from what was happening down there. The lights I had thought I had seen on the water when I was in the car were there, no mistake. I could hear the faint splash of oars and voices. Not English or Welsh but some foreign tongue. I knew without being told it was French. They were coming! The bloated, walking corpses of those who died on the night of the 23rd of February 1797. The French were returning to Carreg Wastad.

I got up to run but Spencer dragged me down again. Strong man, he was. 'Keep quiet!' he hissed.

I struggled. Desperate, I was. 'It's the French!' I almost screamed. 'The dead ones are coming ashore.'

He held onto me. 'It's the French all right,' he said calmly. 'But not dead, Captain. I can assure you of that. Stay where you are. I want you to see this and take note.'

I began to have second thoughts about George Spencer. Giving orders like he was born to it. Not a bit like some of the limp-wristed writers I've met before.

The moon came out again, making it like day. The keel of a boat grated on the pebbles and I saw two men jumping into the surf, while a third backed the boat away from the beach. Behind them, not more than a mile offshore, I could see the shadowy outline of a blacked-out ship. Not a tall-masted frigate from the 1790's but a small, modern cargo vessel. I'd seen plenty like her crossing Cardigan Bay on their way up to Liverpool. Short-sea traders running to the Mediterranean, most of them.

There was nothing ghostly about the men coming ashore, either. French they might be, but they wore very up to date gear; light oilskins, seaboots and woolly hats. None of your old fashioned fancy dress. Both of them were carrying heavy canvas holdalls. Now, I've done a bit of smuggling in my time. Small stuff, of course; whisky and cigarettes from the Irish boats. But this little lot looked as though they were up to something nasty.

The two men passed within ten feet of us, heads down and nattering away in their funny language. Not a very nice looking pair, they were. As soon as they were out of sight, I whispered to Spencer, 'Smugglers, Mister Spencer. What's your interest in this? Are you Customs or Police?'

'Drugs Squad,' he said curtly. 'And, if I'm not mistaken, we've just seen a load of heroin coming ashore. Now let's get back to the car—and, for God's sake, keep quiet. They'll probably be armed.'

I went as quiet as a mouse. No thought of ghosts now. We made it back to the car crawling like Red Indian scouts and me feeling as though I had a dose of the runs coming on. Spencer was breathing hard but as cool as a cucumber, give him his due.

When we were back inside the car and my stomach had settled, I asked him if he was going to try to arrest the men.

He shook his head. 'Not yet. They're only the carriers. Small fry. I want the real villains, the men selling the heroin to the kids on the streets. I want them badly,' he added, raising his voice. Then, he reached under the dashboard and brought out a microphone. '*Night Rider!*' he called briskly. '*Night Rider*, this is *Seagull*. Do you receive?'

A loudspeaker close to my ear crackled into life. 'Loud and clear, *Seagull*. Go ahead.'

Spencer was brief. 'Bandits ashore Carreg Wastad. Heading inland. Follow but do not detain. Over and out!'

'Roger!' came back the answer and the radio fell silent.

It was all great stuff. Seen it on the television plenty of times. I was beginning to enjoy myself. 'Who was that?' I asked, settling back in my seat.

'My inspector. He's got a squad of men in the bushes.' He smiled. 'I think you disturbed them.'

'They disturbed me, Mister,' I grunted.

'Sorry about that, old man. They're a bit heavy footed at times. But I can rely on them to follow the smugglers to the rendezvous, wherever that might be. Shouldn't be surprised if the three Frenchmen Caradog Jenkins said were staying at the Bay Hotel weren't waiting there. Too much of a coincidence for them not to be involved.'

'Why aren't you going after them yourself?' I asked, wondering why he was sitting chatting to me.

Spencer shook his head. 'I daren't show my face. The big boys in drugs don't know me yet and, so long as I stay out of sight, I can fight them. If they ever get to identify me, it's goodbye Chief Inspector George Spencer, for sure.'

I thought he was joking. 'They wouldn't touch you. You're a policeman.'

He laughed out loud. 'Don't you believe it, Captain. They're a ruthless bunch.' Then, he reached forward and switched on the ignition. The engine fired first time.

'Well, bugger me!' was all I could say.

Chief Inspector Spencer winked. 'Sorry about that, Captain. It was the only way I could get you down to the beach.'

★   ★   ★   ★

I watched the papers for three weeks after that but not a word. I heard that the three Frenchmen had disappeared from the Bay Hotel without paying their bill, so it looked as though the police had nabbed them. It was another month before I got to know the full story. I was in the Kings Arms knocking back pints and talking to Caradog Jenkins, when who should walk in but Chief Inspector George Spencer.

'Evening, Mister Jenkins, evening Captain,' he said, just as if he was a regular in every night. He called for a round of drinks. I took beer this time. Ever since that night, I'd gone off the whisky.

There was no talk while we tasted our drinks, then Spencer put down his glass with a sigh. 'Ah well . . . I suppose I owe you chaps an explanation,' he said.

'Too bloody right, you do!' I told him.

He propped his elbows on the bar. 'Right. I'll keep it as short as I can. For more than five years I've been after a gang known to be smuggling heroin into this country in a big way. I had no idea who they were, where they were based or how they got the stuff in. Every way I turned, I came up against a blank wall. The only lead I had was that this particular brand of heroin—and it was a very distinctive type—always appeared on the streets in large quantities on the 24th of February each year. Precisely on the 24th. It was uncanny.'

'The 24th of February?' Caradog said, with his mouth open.

Spencer just nodded and went on. 'For the best part of five years I've had every likely access to the country closely watched throughout the month of February; ports, airports, even railway stations. Closed circuit television, X-ray cameras, sniffer dogs, I've used the lot. Not even a grain of heroin should have got through. Yet it did and as regular as clockwork. The drug was always in the hands of the pushers on the 24th. There was no doubt in my mind the stuff was being landed in some very remote spot and most probably on the night of the 23rd.'

I was so carried away by his tale that I told Caradog to set up a round of drinks. 'How come you connected it with the 'Anniversary'?' I asked Spencer.

He gave a short laugh. 'Quite by chance. My daughter was doing a thesis on Modern Welsh History for her Ph.D. and asked me to collect some books from the library. Amongst them was a small book on the French invasion of 1797. I had always thought our last home match was in 1066 so I was interested enough to read the book. The date of the invasion, 23rd of February, began to ring bells. Then, when I read about the legend of the ghosts of Carreg Wastad and how the locals battened themselves down indoors on the night of the 23rd, I knew I was onto something. Carreg Wastad and the night of the 'Anniversary' seemed the perfect place and time to land a large consignment of illegal drugs.'

'So you were just having us on when you were here on that night back in February,' Caradog said. 'You knew as much about the 'Anniversary' as we did.'

Spencer looked sheepish. 'I will admit to leading you on, but I needed your confirmation. I needed all the information I could get.'

A thought struck me. 'If you ask me,' I said, 'the smugglers started all that talk about ghosts so they could use Carreg Wastad as a landing place. With all of us silly fools with our heads under the blankets, they could do what they liked.'

'You could put it that way, Captain,' Spencer said with a smile. 'But the legend of the ghosts has been around for quite a long time. It's believed the Germans started it during the First World War, when they had plans to land spies at Carreg Wastad. For some reason, the people of Fishguard took the story to heart and kept it alive. The heroin smugglers probably stumbled on it in much the same way as I did.'

Well . . . that made us lot in Fishguard look like right paddies. Over the years, there's been some good fishing lost in Cardigan Bay on the night of 23rd. Not to mention the money Caradog and the other landlords had lost through early closing. No use crying over spilt milk, though. 'Did you get the smugglers, Mister Spencer?' I asked.

He nodded. 'The whole gang, including the men we saw on the beach and the crew of the ship. They were arrested when she put into the Falmouth for stores. She was French as well, by the way.'

'And what about the heroin?'

'We collected the lot. The biggest single haul we've ever had. Worth over ten million pounds on the streets.'

Well that was a relief. I hadn't been able to get those young kids out of my mind for a long time. There was something I couldn't understand, though. 'Why did you drag me into it, Mister Spencer?' I asked. 'You had your own men out there. Why didn't you leave me to go home on the bus, same as I always do?'

'For two reasons,' he said. 'I needed a reliable man to witness the landing; someone not connected with the Force. Also, I thought it high time the ghosts of Carreg Wastad were laid. And what better man to do it than you—a local sea captain?'

My stomach was turning over. 'You'll want me in court, then?'

He finished his drink, and buttoned his coat. 'No need to worry, Captain. My men will look after you. Goodnight, Mister Jenkins, goodnight, Captain. And thank you both.'

When he was gone, Caradog poured me a large whisky without asking. I must have looked in need of it. 'The people around here will miss the 'Anniversary',' he said sadly.

I finished the whisky in one go and my brain began to tick over. 'No reason why they should, is there?' I said, leaning across the bar and lowering my voice. 'I know where I can get hold of a load of duty free brandy. Once a year would be enough. Twenty-third of February. Carreg Wastad. Nice little bit of profit in it for us, Caradog.'

THE OWNER'S CHOICE

Captain Henry Blunt, pipe showering sparks, his red face dripping sweat, paced the confines of his cabin in a towering rage. He stopped abruptly, stamped a fragment of burning dottle into the carpet and pointed his pipe stem in my direction. 'It's all your fault, Mister Idwal Pugh!' he bawled. 'You and your bloody Welsh tricks!'

I ran my fingers through what was left of my thinning hair and groaned. It was bad enough to be going bald at thirty, the hangover was worse but the Old Man doing his Captain Bligh act was the last straw. I smothered a burp and tasted the sewers of Cardiff in my mouth. 'Well, sir,' I said, 'yesterday *was* St. David's Day and you *did* give permission for us to hold a bit of a party.'

The Captain resumed his up and down performance, the loose fittings of the cabin rattling with the agitated passage of his sixteen stones. 'A couple of pints to celebrate some Welsh vicar who's been dead for a thousand years is one thing, but this is just damn ridiculous,' he rumbled. 'Twelve hours after your "bit of party", the whole crew's still stoned out of their minds. What the devil were you drinking, anyway?'

You couldn't help being sorry for Captain Blunt. English, see. No feeling for *Dewi Sant* at all and definitely on the wrong ship, poor chap. The *Penarth Trader* was Cardiff owned and 100 percent Welsh manned. There wasn't a man jack of us that didn't worship regularly at the Arms Park; except Captain Blunt. He'd never tried my Mam's parsnip wine either, so I owed him an explanation. 'Ran out of beer, we did, sir. And, things being what they are on this ship, I had to bring out the parsnip wine. Couldn't let a good party spoil for the want of a drop of something, could I?'

The Old Man halted in mid-stride, a look of disbelief on his face. 'Parsnip wine?' he said. 'Do you mean to tell me that parsnip wine was responsible . . .?' he stopped and nodded his head. 'I see . . . Welsh parsnip wine. That explains it.' He gave

me a worried look. 'How much of this stuff do you carry, for
God's sake? You know this ship's supposed to be dry.'

I coughed discreetly, which I always do before telling a
barefaced lie. 'Truth is, sir, my Mam always puts half a dozen
bottles in my case when I come away. Normally I wouldn't
touch the stuff; it all goes over the side as soon as we get into
deep water. Bloody lethal, it is. But last night was special,
see.' I could see by the blank look in his eyes that I wasn't
getting through to him, so I changed tack. 'You don't have to
worry, sir. The lads are all working this morning. A bit under
the weather but doing their best.'

He had his pipe going again and he was pushing great
clouds of blue smoke towards me. 'All working away like
good little boys, are they?' There was a nasty, sarcastic note
in his voice. 'And the chief Steward and the cook? Do you
happen to know what they're doing, Mister Pugh?'

'Well . . .,' I said cagily. The last I had seen of the pair he
mentioned they were trying to cook bacon and eggs in the
officers' washing machine—at two o'clock in the morning.

The Old Man took a step towards me, blowing smoke in
my face. Deliberate, I think. 'I'll tell you what they're
doing,' he hissed. 'The chief Steward's locked in the toilet
and won't come out because he's frightened of the snakes
and the cook's in the Royal Infirmary with a stomach pump
stuck down his guts. That's what they're doing, Mister!' He
snorted. 'You and your Mam's parsnip wine.'

I gave a sigh of relief. If that was all that was upsetting him
it was easily fixed. Captain Blunt was a food addict and the
thought of missing a meal, or even two, was like asking him
to go on the bridge in his underpants. To be fair, at his age,
you've got to have something to make up for no sex. There's
terrible it must be.

I gave him a sympathetic smile. 'No problem there, sir.
There's a Chinese take-away just outside the dock gates. I'll
send one of the lads up . . .' I broke off. The Old Man was
stroking his nose with the stem of his pipe. A bad sign that.

'Mister Pugh,' he said, making my name sound like a bad
smell, 'if you are capable of such a thing, cast your parsnip
wine-soaked mind back to yesterday. Did I not tell you to get

the ship cleaned up, wash down the gangway, break out new flags?'

'All done before we started the party, sir.' I said smugly. Then I realised what he was going on about and the stale drink rose in my throat again. '*Diawch!* The bloody Owner's coming to dinner tonight.'

The Old Man nodded. 'Exactly, Mister Pugh. Sir Percival Pettigrew is coming to dinner on board this ship. The man who pays my salary and, unfortunately, yours. He's due at six o'clock sharp and is expecting a four-course meal with all the trimmings. During this meal I had intended to put before him certain proposals which would have benefited us all—a ten percent increase in salary for a start.'

I swallowed hard. This was serious. No chief steward, no cook and most of the crew still half-drunk. Sir Percival Pettigrew was as strict TT as they come and he expected his employees to be the same. Drinking on board a Pettigrew ship meant instant dismissal. It went on, of course, but it was a hard job getting a regular supply of booze. On the *Penarth Trader*, if it hadn't been for my Mam and her homemade wine, we would have died of thirst.

'Well, Mister?'

The Old Man was obviously expecting me to come up with something brilliant. 'Chippy makes a good curry, sir,' I tried. 'He used to be in Indian ships, you know . . .'

He was shaking his head even before I finished. 'You'll have to do better than that, Mister. This ship's carpenter couldn't open a tin of baked beans without using a fourteen pound hammer, let alone . . .'

Hammer? My brain stirred sluggishly and then clicked into gear. Dorothy Hammer! Now, there was a girl who could save our bacon, so to speak. My confidence came rushing back. 'It's all right, sir,' I burst out. 'I know where to get hold of a cook at short notice. She'll dish up a meal to make the old . . . er . . . Sir Percival's mouth water.'

Captain Blunt looked at me suspiciously, 'She?'

'Yes, sir. A young lady I happen to know very well. Lives in Cardiff. Very high class cook she is, too.'

He thought for a minute, then said warily. 'How much is this going to cost me?'

'Just the price of a lunch, sir. And a few drinks, of course. The lady likes a little drink, see.'

He grunted and disappeared into his bedroom. My hangover was easing off and I could even manage a smile as I listened to him cursing and banging away at the antique safe he kept in his wardrobe. Things were looking up. A few pints, lunch and Dottie Hammer all on the Old Man was something that happened only once in a lifetime.

I was in for a disappointment. Re-appearing from the bedroom, Captain Blunt handed me a grubby five pound note. 'Mind you bring the change back,' he said, quite serious. 'It's the Company's money.'

Dottie Hammer was where I knew she would be, in the cocktail bar of the *Prince of Wales*, third stool from the right as you come in through the door. The place was half-empty and, as soon as she spotted me, she hitched up her skirt another couple of inches and started fluffing out her long, blonde hair; a natural reaction for Dottie when there's a customer in the offing. Being a bit short-sighted she hadn't recognised me straight off.

'Hullo, Dot. How's business?' I said brightly, sliding onto the stool next to her and getting an eyeful of her gorgeous legs.

Lovely girl, Dottie Hammer. Very young looking and a nice dresser, too. If you didn't know, you'd think she was just down from Cheltenham Ladies—which she wasn't, of course. She was pushing thirty five to the best of my knowledge and her language was something out of the middle of a rugby scrum. 'What the hell are you doing here, Idwal Pugh?' she said as soon as she recognised me. Then, before I could state my case, 'Beat it, sailor boy. No free handouts today.'

She was obviously referring to the one and only time we shared a bed and I had sneaked out at five in the morning without leaving the usual on the dressing table. Broke I was and, besides, I object to paying for something seamen ought to have on the National Health. But business was business with Dottie and she'd never forgiven me.

I took out my wallet and flashed the Company's fiver. 'My shout this time, Dot,' I said magnanimously. 'A few drinks and a nice lunch after. How does that grab you?'

She gave me one of those looks that can kill. 'No bloody grabbing for you, boy. You still owe me ten quid—and a new nightie.'

I'd clean forgotten about the nightie. Inclined to be a bit rough I am after I've been away at sea for a while. I made a quick check of my wallet. 'Tell you what, Dot,' I said with a sick smile. 'I'll take you into M & S and buy you a new nightie as well.' Captain Blunt would have to open up that rusty old safe of his again after this girl had finished with me.

She had her hand on my thigh now and was giving me one of her sexy looks. 'And what do I have to do for all this, darling?' she asked coyly.

I removed her hand, 'Work, Dottie,' I said firmly. 'Work— and not the kind you're thinking of, either. Now listen to me.' She listened.

★   ★   ★   ★

It was nearly four o'clock by the time we got aboard the ship and we were both more than a bit tipsy. I smuggled Dottie into the galley, found her a clean apron and wished her luck. Not that I was leaving much to chance. Before turning to her more profitable way of life, Dottie had been a professional cook.

I found a steward who was practically sober and sent him in to tidy up the saloon. Then I went up to report to the Old Man.

'Just tell me the worst, Mister Pugh,' Captain Blunt growled when I knocked and entered his cabin.

'Not a thing to worry about, sir,' I answered confidently. 'Dinner on the table at six-thirty sharp.'

'I hope for your sake, this woman can cook,' he said, still not convinced.

'The best, sir. Assistant chef at the Prince of Wales Hotel she is, sir.' No harm in using a bit of imagination, is there?

The Old Man looked at me suspiciously. 'Then, why isn't she cooking there tonight, instead of on this ship?' he asked. Give him his due, he wasn't daft.

'Night off, sir,' I lied. But, strictly speaking, I wasn't so far from the truth. Dottie always insisted in having one night off in the week. Union minded, see.

Captain Blunt fished out his pouch and began stuffing shreds of golden tobacco into his pipe. 'Whatever you do,' he said without looking up from his task, 'keep her out of sight. You know Sir Percival won't tolerate women on his ships.'

I nodded agreeement, being quite aware that Sir Percival Pettigrew, apart from being dead set against drink, had a thing about women on ships, too. Mind you, if you'd met his wife you could understand. 'Don't you worry, sir. She'll be invisible,' I said, making for the door.

'And . . . Mister Pugh!'

I turned. 'Yes, sir?'

'It had better be good.'

★   ★   ★   ★

The meal wasn't just good. It was magnificent. I'm usually only partial to plain food but, as I sat there with the fancy courses coming up one after the other, served by a sober steward in clean white jacket, I must admit I was impressed. It was a meal fit for a king—or a cantankerous old shipowner.

Sir Percival sat back at last, his round face glowing. 'Absolutely first class, Captain,' he burbled. 'Where on earth did you pick up such a splendid cook?'

The Old Man disappeared behind his pipe and matches, mumbling something I couldn't catch. Then things began to look serious. Sir Percival turned to me. 'Run along to the galley, Mister Pugh, there's a good chap. Ask the cook to step in here. I'd like to shake his hand.'

I started to get up, wondering if there was anyone on board sober enough to pass off as the cook. Then the decision was taken out of my hands. The saloon door flew open and there was Dottie Hammer, flour on her nose, her blonde hair tucked up under the chef's hat and a soppy smile on her face.

She was a lot more drunk than when I had last seen her. I caught a whiff of my Mam's parsnip wine and I knew why.

The Old Man looked as though he was going to cry and I started calculating my chances of a job in a foreign-flag ship. Then Dottie came waltzing across the saloon, staggering ever so slightly but swinging her hips nicely. She leaned over the table and peered short-sightedly at Sir Percival. The Owner seemed very embarrassed and trying to slide under the table. It got worse. Dottie pinched Sir Percival's cheek and said in a sweet little voice, just a bit slurred, 'So this is where you've been hiding, Percy, you naughty boy. You haven't been to see your little Dottie for weeks.'

Sir Percival seemed near to a stroke. 'Why . . . er . . . hullo, Dorothy,' he managed to squeak. 'I've been . . . er . . . rather busy. Pressure of work, you know.'

Dottie was in his lap by now, nuzzling his ear and completely ignoring the Old Man and me. 'We'll make up for it tonight then, won't we, Percy?' she cooed. 'Dottie's got plenty of your favourite gin at the flat. Oh . . . we'll have a real smashing time . . .'

The Old Man looked at me and I looked at him, then we slipped quietly out of the saloon, leaving them to it.

I've had to tell my Mam not to bother about the parsnip wine any more. Plenty of drink on the *Penarth Trader* now and all out in the open, too.

FLAGGED OUT

'Well, that's the way it is, Captain. The ship has to go and you with it, I'm afraid.' The Fleet Manager carefully placed his cigar in a large onyx ashtray and leaned back in his deep-buttoned hide chair. 'As you are well aware,' he went on expansively, 'British shipping is in the worst doldrums since the nineteen thirties. And you can take it from me, Portman is in as dire straits as the rest.'

Ian Roberts, on the other side of the leather-topped, rosewood desk, sat stunned. Twenty-nine years with Portman Shipping, ten years in command, not a black mark against his name and yet he was about to be given the push. It *had* to be a bad dream. He rummaged in the pockets of his old tweed jacket, found a crushed packet of Silk Cut and lit up with unsteady hands. The first, anxious drag made his head spin, reminding him he had given up smoking three days back. Disgusted with himself, he stubbed out the cigarette in Seb Bullers expensive ashtray and leaned across the desk. 'Are you telling me I'm sacked, Mister Buller?' he asked in a tense voice.

Eyeing the still smouldering cigarette disdainfully, the Fleet Manager retrieved his cigar from the ashtray and puffed importantly. 'They call it redundancy, these days, old man,' he said, waving aside a cloud of Havana-scented, blue smoke. 'There is a difference, you know.'

Roberts, thinking of the unpaid mortgage, brightened. 'Golden handshake?' he asked hopefully.

Buller's florid face disappeared behind the smokescreen. He gave an embarrassed cough. 'Ah . . . not exactly, Captain. I did, of course, raise the question of a severance payment with the Board but Portman is in a severe economic crisis. In my opinion, we'll be lucky to survive. You can rest assured I fought hard for you, old man but there's absolutely nothing in the kitty. Nothing at all.' He brought his chair upright and, with his elbows firmly on the leather facing of the desk top, he steepled his thick fingers like a pontificating bishop. 'You will at least be entitled to something from the Government. A few thousand, or so.' He gave a thin smile. 'Help to keep the wolf from the door, eh?'

Roberts regarded the other man steadily. Sebastian Buller, onetime assistant purser in passenger ships, graduated into management through a spell in Her Majesty's Navy, practised in the art of back-stabbing and social climbing. I know who *you* fought for, Seb Buller, he thought bitterly. And, as for the Government handout, at the going rates for axed master mariners it wouldn't even pay off the bank loan outstanding on his car, let alone the mortgage. He stood up abruptly. 'That's it, then,' he said flatly.

Buller came to his feet smiling, his hand outstretched. 'Good luck, old man,' he began. But Roberts was gone, leaving the Fleet Manager with his hand hanging in midair.

The pavements of Liverpool's aptly named Water Street glistened wet and miserable under a thick curtain of drizzle blown in off the Mersey by a moaning November wind. Although still early afternoon, darkness was setting in and yellow lights already shone from the windows of the offices, where armies of clerks, typists and executives whiled away the closing hours of their working day. Roberts turned up the collar of his raincoat and walked, head down, towards the river. Ignoring the prodding umbrellas of the early leavers, he blundered past the Royal Liver Building, legendary home of the city's shipping past, dodged the splashing cars on the dock road and finally found himself leaning on the stone parapet of the sea wall. He gazed into the gathering dusk, the cold drizzle drifting around him, frosting his faded, brown hair and softening the wrinkles around his tired eyes.

Twenty-nine years ago he had first sailed down this river, he reflected sadly. A fresh-faced, eager cadet, for whom Portman Shipping was the beginning and the end of the world. Twenty-nine years in which he had progressed steadily and conscientiously through the ranks. 3rd Officer at 21, 2nd Officer and nagivator two years later, followed by eight years hard slog as Chief Officer and, finally, to the peak of his profession as captain in command. It had been a good life, often

dangerous and uncomfortable but healthy, active and re-
warding. In return, he had given Portman Shipping twenty-
nine years of professional dedication and complete loyalty.
So why had he been thrown onto the scrap heap? Seb Buller
could call it redundancy if he liked, but there was no getting
away from the truth. Captain Ian Roberts, forty-six years old,
with two young kids in private schools and a five-figure
mortgage to pay off, had been suddenly and unceremoniously kicked out on his backside.

The impatient shriek of a tug's whistle caused Roberts to
turn his head down river. A huge, slab-sided container ship
was manouvering to enter the locks. An ensign of indeter-
minate nationality hung limply on her stern. One thing was
certain—she was not British. Another foreign ship, backed
by speculative money, operating with a sub-standard crew to
a set of rules drawn up to achieve the ultimate in corner-
cutting. Meanwhile, the British merchant fleet doggedly
played the game and sank slowly into oblivion. Roberts
shook his head. There was no justice in today's maritime
world.

He flicked a bead of accumulated drizzle from the end of
his nose and squared his shoulders. Sulking on the banks of
the Mersey crying about what should have been would get
him nowhere. He needed to do something about his own pre-
dicament—and quickly. For a start, he could do worse than
go home, have a hot bath and then talk things over with Liz.
Ten years his junior she might be, but there was a hard competent side to her. She was bound to have some sensible ideas
of how to cope with the mortgage and the school fees. He set
off briskly back towards the city, his spirits rising. Before he
had gone half a dozen paces, he slowed to a halt. No. It
wouldn't be fair to burden Liz with his troubles yet. He
needed time to think.

The *Ship Aground*, in Castle Street, was a pub steeped in
the salty past of Merseyside. The demands of today's hurrying
generation had given rise to the introduction of pub lunches
but the smoke-blackened oak beams, high-backed settles
and copper lanterns set their indelible seal on the place. The

Ship Aground was still a seaman's pub, where the real talk was of the sea and ships.

Roberts found a table in a dark recess of the saloon bar and was drinking alone. Two pints of beer and three large whiskies had only served to deepen his gloom. The awful realisation that he had joined the ranks of the unemployed kept washing over him like breakers on a reef. In one miserable, rain-laden morning, he had gone from Captain Ian Roberts, senior master with one of Britain's oldest shipping companies, professional seaman of high repute, respected member of his local community, to become plain I. Roberts, just another number in the dole queue.

★   ★   ★   ★

The telephone had rung in mid-morning, when Roberts was deep and satisfyingly in the throes of decorating the spare bedroom.

'It's the Office!' Liz called, a worried edge to her voice. When Ian was on leave, an unexpected call from Portman was always a threat to her temporary happiness.

The personnel clerk was evasive, passing only the terse message that the Fleet Manager wished to see Captain Roberts that afternoon. No hint of the reason behind the call but obviously, something important had come up. Roberts was puzzled but not unduly worried. His last voyage had been an uneventful one. No serious mishaps, no groundings, no heavy cargo claims. It was most unlikely, then, he was being hauled up to the Office to answer awkward questions. He whistled tunelessly as he drew his brush deftly along the edge of the window frame, without running as much as a millimetre of paint onto the glass. It had been rumoured that there was a marine superintendent's job going in South-hampton. He was one of the most senior masters and a long way off retiring, so why shouldn't they offer it to him? It would mean all the upset and expense of moving house again, of course, but it *was* a shore job and there were worse places to live than the South Coast. Yes, Roberts decided, carefully removing a loose hair from his brush, he would accept.

The fond dream had become a hideous nightmare and he was now reduced to cowering in the shadows, half-drunk and dully conscious of the heavy weight of his financial commitments bearing down on his shoulders. He had been such a blind fool not to have seen what was coming. The death sentence had been hanging over British shipping for years. Low freights, high taxation, crippling fuel costs, expensive crews. The consequences were inevitable. Yet, he had saddled himself with a huge mortgage, confident that his large and increasing salary was safe into the foreseeable future. Not content with that—he must have been drunk with affluence—he had convinced himself that private education for his children was a justifiable investment. The competent, alert master mariner, who never put a foot wrong at sea, had been caught on a domestic lee shore with all his financial sails aback.

'Enjoying your leave, Ian?' a cheerful voice broke into his reverie.

Roberts looked up, prepared to give vent to his disgruntled feelings. Then, he recognised the tall, wiry figure standing over him and got sheepishly to his feet. He held out his hand and forced a quick smile. 'Hullo, George. Nice to see you again.'

Captain George Mountjoy's keen, grey eyes, half-hidden under his enormous bushy eyebrows, made a searching appraisal of the other man as they shook hands. He refused the offer of a drink and sat down. 'You in trouble, young Ian?' he asked, without preamble.

Roberts resumed his seat and lifted his glass so that the light sparkled on the amber liquid. 'Nothing I can't handle, George,' he said, his eyes not leaving the glass.

Mountjoy snorted. 'Come on, out with it, man! There's something wrong. It's written all over your face.'

Lowering his glass without drinking, Roberts faced the older man. 'How's retirement agreeing with you, George?' he said evasively.

Mountjoy was angry. 'Bugger my retirement! I want to know what's happened to you.'

Roberts sighed. He had spent many satisfying years as junior officer under the command of George Mountjoy. He had come to learn that, although the Captain was a hard and demanding taskmaster, he was a fair and understanding man. When he had retired at 65, he had been sorely missed in the ships of Portman Shipping but, although no longer sea-going, he kept in touch with affairs and was always ready to give sound advice when required. Roberts now found it easy to unload his troubles onto this shrewd, white-haired old man, who sat listening quietly, nodding in agreement and interjecting with a brief question from time to time.

When Roberts had finished, Mountjoy sat back and, pro-ducing a battered, flat tin, unhurriedly rolled himself a smoke. Finally, when the ends of the cigarette were tamped down and free from loose shreds of tobacco, he lit up and blew a thin stream of smoke at the yellowed ceiling. 'It was bound to come, Ian,' he said softly. 'You know I've got no time for Seb Buller but he was right. British shipping is on its last legs. Nobody's job is safe.'

Roberts slammed his glass to the table with a crash. 'But twenty-nine years, George! Half a lifetime of good service and all I get is a limp handshake and a 'Sorry, old man'' from a fat, jumped-up purser whose idea of a hard day's work is a three hour lunch with the General Manager. Not even a few thousand to ease me on my way—and what I'll get from the Government is peanuts. It won't even pay the kids' school fees for a year.'

Mountjoy shrugged. 'That's the way it goes, Ian.'

'But why, George? What about the dockers, the miners, the steelworkers? Thirty, forty thousand just to walk away from their jobs without making a fuss. And what happens to the merchant seamen? Kicked in the teeth and told to piss off just like it's always been. You'd think we were a social disease instead of the lifeline of the country.'

Captain Mountjoy held out a restraining hand. 'Calm down, lad. You're shouting, and that won't alter things. It's a fact of life that it's cheaper to ship cargo in foreign bottoms than British ones these days.' He leaned forward across the table. 'Do you realise, you can charter an old Panamanian tramp for not much more than the cost of her bunkers? We both know who's to blame for this but there's big money involved. So don't look to the shipowner or the Government to help you out. They've got you by the balls and they know it.'

Roberts nodded. Of course he had been aware of these facts but he had been refusing to face up to them. So long as he had been in command of a ship, he had felt inviolate. 'What the hell am I going to do now, George?' he asked. 'I can't afford to be out of work.'

'Find another job, then,' Mountjoy said unhelpfully.

Roberts gave a cynical laugh. 'You're joking! Where would I find another command?'

'Foreign flag. Plenty of those ships looking for good, experienced masters. Some of them may be a bit rough but it's a job.'

Tossing off the remains of his drink, Roberts got to his feet. 'No thanks, George. I've served under the Red Ensign all my life and I'm not likely to join the mercenaries now. That would be betraying my country.'

'Your country has betrayed you, Ian.' Mountjoy called softly after the younger man as he left the bar.

★   ★   ★   ★

Ten days later, frustrated, dejected and weary, Ian Roberts slouched into the *Ship Aground*. Captain Mountjoy was already seated in one of the alcoves, a half-finished pint before him. 'No luck, Ian?' he asked, when Roberts had collected his drink from the bar and joined him.

Roberts shook his head. 'Not a damned thing! I must have tried every shipping company in the country. I'm sick and tired of writing, telephoning and knocking on doors. I've worn out at least one pair of shoes tramping around Liverpool alone. Nobody's as much as offered me a Mate's job, let alone a command.'

Mountjoy hunched his shoulders and took a frugal sip at his beer. 'Portman's gone bust, you know?' he said without looking up. 'Sold out to the Arabs, so they say.'

'Yes . . . I heard. That means Seb Buller's out of a job as well. I hope the bastard gets the same reception as I've had.'

'Not him,' Mountjoy said with a short laugh. 'He's got friends in the right places.' He rubbed his chin and regarded Roberts earnestly. 'Do you really want a job, Ian?'

It was Roberts' turn to laugh. 'George, I'm bloody near skint! If I don't get something soon, I'll have the bailiffs in on me.'

The familiar flat tin and cigarette papers came out. 'If it's that bad, you'll take a foreign flag, then?'

Roberts turned his head away, ashamed to meet the old man's eyes. 'I don't seem to have any choice, George. Have you heard of something going?'

The tin snapped shut and Mountjoy struck a match. 'India Buildings, fourth floor,' he said, drawing deeply on the thinly rolled cigarette. 'Pan-Islamic's looking for a master. Mention my name and the job's yours.'

A phone call to Pan-Islamic Shipping confirmed the vacancy was still open and, within twenty-four hours, Ian Roberts found himself taking the lift to the fourth floor of India Buildings.

He stepped out into the corridor, hesitated, and turned right, following the prominent Pan-Islamic signs. Approaching the glass panelled door with its alien green and white flags, his footsteps slowed. Beyond that door lay a final and irrevocable decision. He realised that, once accepted into Pan-Islamic, he would be deserting the British flag for good. He would be breaking a long tradition set up by his father and his grandfather before him, both master mariners serving their country in the quiet ways of the sea. His father, Captain Tom Roberts, had perished with his ship in the Second World War, along with 30,000 other British merchant seamen. Would he not be desecrating the memory of his father and all those brave men who had given their lives for a principle? It was not too late to turn back. He could give the British companies another try. Liz would stand by him. They would manage the mortgage and the other bills somehow. It might not be a bad thing if the kids did switch to a comprehensive. Something was bound to turn up before long. On the other hand, he

could be out of a ship for years. How much did the dole run to
these days? Roberts squared his tie and pushed open the door
marked Pan-Islamic Shipping.

'Captain Roberts to see the Fleet Manager,' he declared
crisply, in answer to the receptionist's raised eyebrows. She,
at least, was English. A good start.

The girl smiled pleasantly and consulted a paper on the
desk before her. 'Go right in Captain Roberts,' she said, indicating a door behind her. 'He's expecting you.'

Roberts took a deep breath and crossed the deep-pile carpet
to the door labelled *Fleet Manager*. He knocked firmly and
went in.

The interior of the room was not at all what he had expected.
It was neither seedy nor ostentatious. It could well have been
the Fleet Manager's lair in the offices of any one of a dozen
British shipping companies. The furniture was functional
chrome and black leather, a large map of the world occupied
the whole of one wall, while prints of ships long gone decor-
ated the others. The big, leather-topped desk was littered
with papers and the inevitable telex machine chattered away
in a corner near the window.

As Roberts moved further into the room, a strangely familiar
figure turned from the telex machine, carefully placed his
cigar in the onyx ashtray on the desk and advanced with his
hand outstretched. 'Welcome to Pan-Islamic, Captain Roberts!'
Sebastian Buller boomed.

IN THE WAKE OF MATTIE JENKINS

The trouble really started when Captain Ebenezer Howells decided to enter the matrimonial field for the second time.

The first Mrs. Howells, strict Chapel and, throughout her sinless, furniture-polishing life, totally unversed in the fine arts of sensuality, had succumbed after a short illness when the Captain was in his sixtieth year. He was left with a large and empty house, many thousands in the bank and an acute awareness of things unachieved in the sexual realm.

Most men of the Captain's age would have been content to take up golf or the good works of the Lord, perhaps relying on a discreet collection of pornography to while away the lonely nights. Not so Ebenezer Howells. Urged on by the uncomfortable ache in his loins, he searched the villages surrounding his native Aberfach for a replacement Mrs. H. Being thin to the point of emaciation, balding and noticeably short in stature, his task was not an easy one. To be sure, several elderly matrons shook their mothball-scented skirts at him but the seafarer, having tasted the succulent, cheongsamed delights of the Far East, was not to be fobbed off with matrimony accompanied by a dark moustache, 44-inch hips and rheumatoid arthritis. His joy was therefore great when he came upon the comely but not over-intelligent Mattie Jenkins who, coincidentally, was on the lookout for a secure position in society. Long of limb, full of breast and just nineteen years old, Mattie was the perfect altar of Venus on which a man forty years her senior might happily self-destruct.

Sustained by the long years of enforced sexual abstinence, the Captain survived the brief honeymoon and, in the week following, strove manfully to disprove the popular theory that a man's virility decreases with age. It was only in the closing days of his period of shore leave that he began to realise he was on a hiding to nothing. While the delectable Mattie blossomed into demanding maturity, the Captain developed a bad back, a hacking cough and the early symptoms of cardiovascular degeneration. It was not surprising then, that having one day found escape from the insatiable nymphet in the outside lav, he decided he must (a) give up smoking, (b) forego the comfort of alcohol and (c) embark on a vigorous programme of exercises in order to revitalise his flagging body. This radical change of life-style, he firmly resolved, would be carried out on his very next voyage to sea. The clean, salt air, aided by self-denial and the occasional good sweat, would make Ebenezer Howells young again.

★   ★   ★   ★

The *Maid of Pembroke*, 6350 tons gross and the pride of the fleet of Jones, Thomas and Jacobs (Shipowners), Cardiff, made her way lazily across the long swells of the Bay of Biscay. She was twenty-four hours out of Swansea, bound for Abu Riaz on the Red Sea coast of Saudi Arabia.

Boatswain Tom Madoc, six feet four inches, wide-shouldered and with a jaw chiselled out of Preseli granite, knocked loudly and entered the Captain's office with a purposeful tread.

Captain Ebenezer Howells looked up and pulled aside his paperwork. 'Come in, Tom,' he said warmly. 'What can I do for you?'

Howells and his boatswain, both born and reared in Aberfach, were of different generation but, as is usually the case in small communities, they had family ties. Tom Madoc and Mattie—the second Mrs. Howells—were in fact third cousins and, in their schooldays, had been very close; so close that Mattie's father had once threatened to take a shotgun to Tom if he ever caught them 'up to their tricks' in his barn again. Captain Howells was, of course, not aware of this side of the relationship.

Tom Madoc shifted uncomfortably. 'Official complaint from the crew, sir.'

Captain Howells raised his eyebrows. 'Complaint, Tom? Whatever have they got to complain about? They get the best of everything on this ship.'

Madoc felt even more uncomfortable. The *Maid of Pembroke* was a good feeding ship and the discipline was nothing to get upset about. But this was different. 'It's about the beer, sir. They haven't had any since we sailed.'

It was the Captain's turn to experience discomfort. 'Ah . . . yes, Tom,' he began, reaching for his cigarettes which, of course, were not there—the last packet having been hurled into the muddy waters of the Bristol Channel in a fit of righteous dedication. 'Ah . . . yes,' he said again, stilling his searching fingers. 'I wanted to talk to you about that, Tom.'

Madoc nodded warily. The old bugger was up to something for sure.

'Well . . . it's like this, Tom,' the Captain went on. 'You know how there's been a lot of talk lately about alcoholism at sea. The doctors say the drink is killing seamen off like flies. So I thought . . . well, I thought it might be a good idea if we went 'dry' for a voyage. Just to see how it works, of course,' he added hastily.

Madoc had the distinct feeling he'd been belted with a piece of dunnage. 'You mean you didn't buy any beer for the voyage?' he asked incredulously. The Old Man must be out of his mind.

Captain Howells smoothed down his thinning, grey hair with a firm hand. 'It's just poison, Tom. They'll be much better off without it. Of course, I stocked up with plenty of minerals . . .'

'Minerals!' Madoc echoed. 'For Christ's sake! What am I going to tell the lads? There's seven-pint-a-day men down in that messroom, Captain.'

'It's for their own good, Tom. They'll be grateful to me in the end. You mark my words.'

There seemed to be surprisingly little gratitude in the air when Madoc broke the news in the crew messroom ten minutes later.

Arthur Harris, senior able seaman and self appointed shop steward, was quick off the mark. 'It's a bloody cheek!' he declared angrily, hitching his belt up over his sagging belly. 'Interfering with our democratic rights, that's what it is.' With difficulty, he mounted a wooden crate which had once held bottles of brown ale and addressed the assembly of sailors, firemen and stewards. 'I say we do something about it lads! It's positive action we need!'

For once, his militancy, usually scoffed at, was greeted with a chorus of assent. Even the tiny minority of teetotalers present were moved to protest. Such is the power of alcohol.

Harris was encouraged beyond all expectations. 'Right then, brothers,' he went on briskly. 'There's only one way to deal with that stingy old sod up top. I propose we call a strike. No beer, no work, I say. Let's have a show of hands on that, brothers.'

There was no doubt about the result of the vote. A sea of hands, backed up by cries of 'Hang the bastard!' decisively carried the day.

Tom Madoc decided it was time for a bit of sense to be talked. He took his stance in the centre of the room, hands on hips, legs spread against the roll of the ship.

'You keep out of this, Bos'un!' Harris shouted angrily.

Madoc held up a warning hand. 'Shut up and sit down, Arthur!' he growled. He then let his gaze wander around the messroom, resting on each belligerent face in turn. Within seconds, the place was as quiet as a country churchyard. Madoc raised his voice. 'Now, lads. Think about what you're doing. This ship is at sea and striking at sea is mutiny, remember.'

'That old rubbish went out with Nelson,' Arthur Harris spluttered, the fag in the corner of his mouth waggling energetically. 'We've got our rights these days, haven't we lads?' He looked around him expectantly.

Again shouts of approval but muted now. A small voice at the back of the room cautioned, 'Tom's right about the mutiny bit, though.'

Madoc let out a sigh of relief and moved onto firmer ground. 'You all read the Articles before you signed—or should have done. You agreed to obey the lawful commands of the Master. And, if Captain Howells says you can't have beer, well that's that. No argument.' He paused and looked pointedly at a fuming Arthur Harris. 'Forget all this daft talk about strike—unless you want to end up in jail when we get to Saudi. Any of you ever been in an Arab jail?' Without waiting for an answer, he elbowed his way to the door, barking his shins on an unseen chair as he went out. The messroom was in its usual state of semi-darkness.

★   ★   ★   ★

It was blowing hard on deck when, the next evening, Tom Madoc found a quiet corner and lit a cigarette, cupping the match in his hands. He was avoiding the messroom. The talk in there was still about drink—or the lack of it. It was a pitful sight to see grown men crying for their booze. Enough to make even a moderate drinker like himself thirsty, too. A momentary image of a cool, foaming pint of dark ale crossed his mind, and he licked his salt-cracked lips.

'There's a nice night it is, Bos'un.' Uninvited, the boiler-suited figure of Will Price, ship's electrician had joined him in the shelter of the deckhouse.

Madoc bristled. He had no love for this sly South Walian. 'It'd be a damn sight nicer if you'd fix those bloody lights in the messroom,' he said sourly, rubbing his still bruised shin.

Price picked at his nose and whined, 'You know I'm always up to me bleeding eyes in work . . .'

'Oh . . . give over, Willy,' Madoc interrupted. 'You've never done a day's work since you joined this ship. You don't even wake up until the bar opens.'

Price gave him a hurt look. 'You don't know the half,' he moaned. 'The old Chief's always after me . . . And, talking about the bar, you wouldn't happen to have a little drop of something in your cabin, would you, Tom?'

Madoc shook his head. 'Nothing for you, Willy—or anyone else, for that matter.' Price was a near-alcoholic and the introduction of prohibition on board the *Maid of Pembroke* must have been a terrible shock to his system. Serve you right, thought Madoc, not without a certain amount of satisfaction.

Price sniffled. 'It's not right,' he said. 'Doing hard working men out of their only little bit of pleasure. No wonder the crew's going to walk off when we get to Abu Riaz.'

Madoc came alert. 'Who told you that?'

'I just happened to be working in the messroom,' Price said slyly. 'Lot of talk going on in there.'

'Fixing the lights, were you?'

'Well . . . not exactly. Big job, that. Anyway . . . I heard Arthur Harris telling the rest of the lads that, because of the Articles, they wouldn't be able to strike at sea, so the best thing to do was to walk off when we get to port. Plenty of support he got, too.'

Tom Madoc rubbed his chin. It was high time he and Captain Howells had a serious talk.

Captain Howells was completing his third circuit of the boat deck when Madoc tracked him down.

'Morning, Tom,' Howells gasped, stopping in front of the boatswain but continuing to jog on the spot. His face was the colour of a freshly boiled lobster and his remaining strands of hair—usually carefully arranged to cover his balding head—hung in an untidy grey curtain over his right ear. He came to a sudden, jarring halt. 'Nothing like a bit of hard exercise to keep you fit, eh Tom?' he wheezed. 'Do some of you young boys the world of good.'

Madoc waited for the Captain to recover from a violent fit of coughing before he spoke. 'I'd like a word with you about the crew, sir,' he said ominously.

Captain Howells beamed. 'Want me to organise some exercises for them, do they? That's the ticket, Tom! I told you they would thank me for getting all that old beer out of their systems.'

'No jogging for them,' Madoc said, shaking his head. 'And they want their beer back or we'll have a strike on our hands when we get to port.'

Captain Howells resumed running on the spot. 'Nonsense,' he puffed. 'It's just withdrawal symptoms, Tom. They'll soon get over that. Another week and I'll start cutting back on the cigarettes. Filthy habit, that!' Then, like a vintage car slipping into gear, he shot off, elbows going like pistons, baggy shorts flapping against his thin legs.

'They'll bloody murder you, Ebenezer Howells!' Madoc called after him. But the Captain was already out of earshot.

Two days later, the *Maid of Pembroke* berthed in Abu Riaz, a modern well-found port but, in true Arabian tradition, hot, dusty and alcohol free. As soon as the ropes were out, the crew, led by a grim-faced Arthur Harris, stormed down the gangway and lined up on the quay. The strike was on.

Captain Howells was furious. 'I'll have the lot of them put behind bars!' he roared at Tom Madoc, who had once more been called to the Captain's office.

'That would hold the ship up for sure,' Madoc argued. 'Why don't you at least talk to them, sir?'

The Captain's eyebrows shot up. 'Talk to them? Why should I talk to them? I am Master of the ship and I will not be dictated to by my crew!' he fumed.

'At the moment, you haven't got any crew,' Madoc pointed out. 'They're all sitting on the quay.'

Several hours passed before Captain Howells, subdued but unrepentant, agreed to receive a delegation from his disgruntled crew. A sun-blistered, perspiring Arthur Harris presented himself, backed up by two of the more vociferous members of the deck compartment. Tom Madoc was called in, ostensibly as a witness but, in his own opinion, to protect old Ebenezer from harm.

Captain Howells decided to adopt a fatherly approach. 'Now, boys,' he said genially, when they were all assembled in his office, 'I'm sure we can sort this thing out like sensible people.' He flashed his ill-fitting dentures. 'We're not like these Arabs, are we? Always fighting with each other, they are.' He singled out Arthur Harris, changing his tone. It was schoolmaster to small boy, now. 'Arthur, I am surprised at you; leading the men in a rebellion against the master of the ship. It's not like you at all, Arthur.'

Arthur Harris took exception to being talked down to. He drew himself up to his full five feet four inches. 'I 'ave been instructed by my h'executive,' he began importantly. The two delegates flanking him looked embarrassed.

'Get on with it, Arthur,' Madoc prompted impatiently.

Harris gave the boatswain a look of pure hatred and then addressed the Captain. 'It's like this, Cap'n,' he said sulkily. 'The lads say, ''No beer, no work''—it's as simple as that.

We've withdrawn our labour until such time as we get our democratic rights, see.' Gaining confidence from the sound of his own voice, he leaned forward and planted his large hands on the Captain's desk. 'Either you come up with some beer or the ship doesn't sail—and that's definite!'

Captain Ebenezer Howells, mild man though he might be, was not one to be threatened, especially by one of his crew. He erupted to his feet, causing the startled shop steward to fall back quickly. 'Don't you bloody threaten me, Arthur Harris!' he roared, drenching all present with a fine spray of spittle. 'I'll bloody well hang you from the yardarm of this ship!'

Tom Madoc grabbed Harris by the shirt as he was about to leap over the desk, murder in his eyes. It was a classic case of industrial relations gone wrong.

Suddenly, Captain Howells sat down heavily and looked around him sadly. 'There's gratitude for you,' he said, addressing no one in particular. 'I've always tried to do my best for my crew. And when I try to lead them into a better, healthier way of life, what do I get? A load of abuse.' He sighed heavily and looked up at Harris. 'Now, look here, Arthur. I'll give you one more chance. Bring the men back on board and I'll let bygones be bygones. What about that?'

'What about the beer?' an uncowed Harris demanded.

'Beer?' the Captain asked vaguely, seemingly having forgotten the subject of the meeting. 'Ah . . . yes . . . the drink. Well . . . we'll see about that when we get back to Cardiff.'

'You'll buy some here . . . or else,' Harris said aggresively.

Captain Howells shook his head. 'No drink in this place, Arthur,' he said firmly. 'They are Moslems, see. Heathens they may be, but they've got the right idea about drink.' He began to shuffle through the papers on his desk. 'Now, away you go, Arthur,' he said briskly without looking up. 'It won't do you people any harm to drink lemonade for another couple of weeks.'

It took the three of them to half-carry the demented Arthur Harris out of the office. ''I'll fix you, you bloody old baby snatcher!' he screamed, as he was manouvered struggling through the doorway. Captain Howells, white in the face, was left clicking his teeth at the whole, sorry indignity of the thing.

The last of the cargo was discharged that night but the *Maid of Pembroke* did not sail. The crew, cold and hungry but determined, patiently sat it out on the hard concrete of the quay.

At ten o'clock next morning, Captain Howells sent for his boatswain. 'Look here, Tom!' he burst out, as soon as Madoc entered the office. 'I want you to go down and talk some sense into those men. This ship should have sailed more than twelve hours ago. Head Office will be furious.'

Madoc decided it was high time he made use of their connection by marriage, however tenuous. 'Now you listen to me, Ebenezer Howells,' he said earnestly. 'You and your stupid ideas about health and efficiency, or whatever you call it, have made a mess of this ship. Go without beer, if you want to. Jog up and down the boat deck as much as you like, but don't expect everyone else to join in. Some people just don't like it, see?'

Captain Howells fidgeted in his seat, went red in the face, but remained silent.

Encouraged, Tom Madoc went on. 'Now . . . if you want your crew back on board, you've got to get hold of some beer. I know you can't buy it officially in this place but there's bound to be a black market. Let's get the ship's chandler down and see what he can do, eh?'

Surprisingly, Captain Howells nodded and said calmly, 'All right, Tom. I'll see to it.'

Madoc left the Captain's office with a vague feeling of uneasiness. It had all gone too smoothly.

Within two hours, a small lorry drew up alongside the ship and fifty unmarked, cardboard cartons were discreetly loaded on board. Customs officers patrolling the quay took no interest in the highly suspicious activity. Either a miracle had been wrought or somebody's palm had been heavily greased. The last carton up the gangway was closely followed by a smirking Arthur Harris at the head of his men. The *Maid of Pembroke* sailed from Abu Riaz within the hour.

A victory party was held that night in the crew messroom. Carton after carton of 'Strike Beer', as it had been dubbed, was carried in ceremoniously and placed on the long table. There was laughter, back-slapping and shouts of self-congratulation. Evil-smelling Arab cigars added to the dense cigarette smog threatening to blot out the feeble deckhead lights.

Tom Madoc was content to sit quietly in his usual corner. The messroom was back to its normal, boozy, cheerful self. You had to hand it to Ebenezer Howells; he knew how to fix things. But how had he managed it? Madoc picked up his bottle and examined it in the dim light. It certainly looked like beer. The writing on the label was in Arabic, of course, so that didn't tell him anything. He levered off the top and poured. It was beer, all right. Pale brown, a good head on it and—he took a long swig—it tasted like beer! Not much of a kick in it but it would do.

At that very inopportune moment, Willy Price, filled with zeal and anticipation of the ending of the terrible drought, cleared the earth that had been dimming the messroom lights for longer than anyone present could remember. It was as though the sun had just risen after a long, dark night.

Tom Madoc came to the conclusion that he didn't much care for the new dawn. The harsh lights showed up the smoke-stained paintwork, the oil marks on the deck, deposits of food ingrained into the table top. A lot of work to be done here. To an inquisitive Arthur Harris, the sudden brightness revealed the small print on the label of his bottle of . . . *non-alcoholic beer.*

A room packed with boisterous, laughing seamen turned quickly into an angry, buzzing hornet's nest.

They do say Ebenezer Howells was picked up by a passing fishing boat and is now a parson in South America. As for Tom Madoc and Mattie Howells, nee Jenkins,—her father having passed on—they enjoy many long, happy hours in the barn without fear of interruption. Unfortunately, Tom is developing a bad back, a hacking cough and the early symptoms of cardiovascular degeneration. Beer and cigarettes are out.

ACCOUNT SETTLED

The lounge bar of the *Mariners Arms* was packed with the cream of Porthgwaun's lunchtime drinkers; gentleman farmers, auctioneers and solicitors standing shoulder to shoulder in red-faced harmony. The buzz of well-bred conversation, the clink of Waterford brandy snifters and the hanging curtain of cigar smoke gave the place an air of unashamed self-indulgence.

Captain Huw Powell, wedged in at the fireplace end of the polished oak bar, was the odd man out. This rural fleshpot held no solution to his problems. He was aware that his time would be far better used walking the country lanes and breathing the clear air. In the preceding two hours, he had eaten lavishly, consumed at least half a bottle of whisky and demolished, one after another, a full packet of twenty cigarettes. Yet no relief. The crushing weight still lay across his shoulders like a dead man.

'Is it *that* bad, Huw?' his companion asked, watching him anxiously. Portly, bald-headed Ben Williams, somehow impervious to a lifetime of pub lunches, was Powell's agent in the port and also his best friend.

Powell shrugged and forced a wry smile. 'It could be worse, Ben. Nothing you can help with, anyway. Drink up. It's my round.'

Ben Williams shook his head sadly and fell silent as the dour-faced landlord refilled their glasses.

'You heard about the mermaid?' the landlord asked, re-capping the bottle. No fancy measures in the *Mariners.*

Receiving no answer from his customers, the landlord continued. 'Seen in the bay last night, she was. Plain as day.'

Why is it that we Welsh are possessed of such fertile imaginations? Powell thought, as he eased his way through the crush towards the nearest window, leaving Ben Williams to suffer the monologue.

A glance through the window at the lowering clouds confirmed his fear that the weather was building up into something nasty and he felt again the urgent pull of his ship. Lying alongside in the small, poorly protected harbour of Porthgwaun, the *Sarah James* would be dangerously vulnerable in a gale of wind. She needed him. Powell swirled the remains of his drink around in the bottom of his glass and resolved to leave the warm bosom of this pub after just one more. First, there was the other problem to face up to and the whisky *did* help.

By and large, his marriage to Bethan had been a better than average union. Not always harmonious; but what honest marriage ever was? His frequent absences at sea—painful at times but willingly accepted by both parties—had kept alive their interest in each other, so that each homecoming had about it the freshness of a honeymoon renewed. Long before the end, love had given way to a deeper and seemingly indestructible relationship. Ironically, the wedge that finally split them apart had been their only child, Catrin.

Inheriting Powell's stubborn streak and her mother's dark beauty, Catrin, in tune with her contemporaries in a mindless age, had been kicking hard against parental restraint since entering her teens. Powell had to admit the child—and at eighteen she was still a child in his eyes—had suffered a confused upbringing. While he was away at sea, Catrin and her mother had lived in a cocooned world of feminine harmony, with Bethan giving in too soon and too often. He had become the ogre; the discipline-orientated stranger who rode roughshod through their cosy women's nest every six months or so.

Catrin's tantrums and Bethan's excuses became a regular feature of his brief periods at home. As the years went by, mother and daughter grew closer together and Powell found himself all but excluded from their tight little world. Inevitably, the friction between he and Bethan increased until their only means of communication lay in heated argument. But Powell would not back down. In his own mind, he knew he was right and Bethan wrong. He was sickened by his daughter's outrageous behaviour, her long-haired, pot-smoking boyfriends and the wild parties she lived for.

Things had come to a head six months ago, during his last leave. Catrin had arrived home in the early hours of the morning obviously drunk. Powell, who had also been drinking steadily that night, was easily able to work up a rage that culminated in a bitter slanging match between himself and his daughter. He had called her a 'cheap little slut' and followed up with a stinging backhander across her face. He might just have well stirred up a hornet's nest. The three-cornered row that developed ended with Bethan hurling her wedding ring at him with a scream of, 'Get out of this house, you hypocritical, domineering bastard!' Suddenly sober, he left without bothering to pack his things.

From that day on, he had neither seen nor spoken to either of them. Ben Williams had kept him informed of their movements as best he could. From Ben he learned that, three months after the awful row, Bethan had sold up the house and moved to Pencwm, a market town ten miles inland from Porthgwaun. She had taken a job in a local bank, while Catrin continued her life of senseless dissipation. Although the separation seemed final and complete, Powell could not bring himself to sue for divorce or put them completely out of his mind.

It was late afternoon, and already growing dark, before Powell was able to tear himself away from the soothing atmosphere of the *Mariners Arms*. Guiltily, he hurried down the long, bramble-lined lane leading to the harbour. Spiteful flurries of rain slammed at him, chasing away the cobwebs of alcohol from his brain. His feet rang hollowly on the wooden boards as he half-ran along the jetty, head down into the wind. He was conscious of passing a rusty trawler tugging nervously at her moorings and his concern for his own ship deepened. The small harbour was protected by two curving, stone breakwaters but a long swell, running ahead of the approaching storm, was already finding its way through the entrance.

The *Sarah James* was the only other occupant of the harbour, berthed at the seaward end of the jetty. Powell was relieved to find her riding easily on her fenders, with extra ropes out fore and aft. Tom Baird, the 1st Mate came on deck as Powell vaulted over the bulwark. 'Blow coming up, sir,' Baird called. 'I've doubled the moorings.'

Powell nodded agreement and cast his eye around his command, critically surveying the clean, uncluttered decks. The *Sarah James* was not a ship to turn heads. She was a mere two thousand five hundred tons—little more than a coaster—and twenty years long in the tooth to boot, but Powell ran her as tight as he had run the big cargo liners in the days before his drinking problems had arisen.

'Just keep a close eye on things, Mister,' he grunted irritably. 'I've no wish to be called out of my bed in the middle of the night with the ship adrift in the harbour.' Without waiting for answer or comment, he turned on his heel and headed aft. Baird's eager, boyish face, beneath a mop of overlong hair, did nothing to ease Powell's disgruntled mood. In the big ships, his chief officer had always been a man of maturity and experience. Being understudied by a kid of twenty five was a frightening reminder of how low he had sunk.

Powell sensed something was wrong as soon as he crossed the threshold of his day cabin. Both portholes were open, their curtains whipping in the rising wind. Patches of wet stood out on the threadbare carpet covering the deck of the small room. He shivered. The cabin was cold—unnaturally cold. With quick movements, he slammed shut the ports and hardened down the dogs. Then he became aware of the strong, salty odour of fish hanging in the air. Silently, he cursed his absent steward for the open ports and the neighbouring trawler for the stink of her cargo.

Shrugging out of his coat, he made a closer examination of the wet patches on the carpet. His hackles rose. What he had first seen as puddles of rain blown in through the open ports were now revealed as wet footprints leading across the carpet in the direction of his bedroom. The prints were small—a child perhaps—but an intruder, nevertheless. With a frown creasing his forehead, Powell came up on the balls of his feet and crossed quietly to the open door.

The Captain's bedroom of the *Sarah James*, due to a rare moment of generosity experienced by the shipowner, was fitted out to something resembling passenger ship standards. The elm panelled bulkheads and matching handmade furniture fell only just short of opulence, while the low, divan bed was a refreshing departure from the traditional seaman's bunk. It was this bed that claimed Powell's immediate and startled attention. Lying still on the bright red and green counterpane was a naked woman.

Powell crossed silently to the bed and stook looking down at the intruder. His annoyance gave way to fascination. He was no stranger to the unclothed female body; he had seen them all, from New York to Nagasaki but this one was something special. Young—not yet out of her teens, he guessed. She lay on her side with one small, exquisite breast resting in the curve of her arm. Her skin was flawless, white alabaster, her hair fine, sun-brown silk, flowing down across her shoulders and reaching almost to her tight, rounded bottom. In spite of the chill in the air, her beauty was enough to bring an uneasy sweat to his brow.

He moved in closer. She was fast asleep. Or was she dead? The pallor of her skin and the absence of any sign of breathing suddenly frightened him. He reached out and touched her shoulder. She was indeed as cold as death itself. With panic coursing through his veins, he took her wrist, feeling for a pulse.

The movement under his searching fingers was no more than the nervous flutter of a tiny bird's wings, but at least she was alive. As Powell let out his pent-up breath, her eyes flickered open. They were cold eyes; the cold grey of a storm-washed winter's sky. With cat-like ease, she sat up, hugging her knees and covering her nakedness with her own body. Unlike her eyes, her smile was warm and loaded with invitation.

Powell stepped back warily. Dangerous ground. The girl was young, attractive, unashamedly sensual. The offer in her smile could not be mistaken. 'What are you doing on my ship?' he asked gruffly, covering his embarrassment.

She avoided his gaze. 'Waiting for you.' Her voice was soft and hesitant. No invitation there.

Uncertain, Powell waited until she looked up again. The cold, calculating look, the provocative parting of her full lips. His nostrils twitched, catching the pungent reek of raw fish hanging in the air. Almost reluctantly, he accepted his first assessment of the girl's intentions. Dockside whores were becoming younger and prettier every day and, by the smell of her, this one was hot-foot from plying her trade aboard the fishing trawler further up the jetty. 'Get dressed and get off my ship!' he flung over his shoulder as he strode back into his day-cabin.

With shaking hands, he rummaged in the drink cabinet until he found a bottle of dark rum two thirds full. He poured a stiff tot and threw it down his throat in one quick gulp. The neat spirit hit the spot with the effect of a fire-storm. His hands grew still but his temper continued to surge. He would crucify young Baird for this. Allowing a cheap tart to wander on board was one thing but giving her free reign of the master's bedroom was downright bloody incompetence.

Powell poured himself a generous refill and crossed to forward facing port, where he stood watching the whitecaps roughen up the leaden waters of the harbour. With the barometer taking a nosedive, it might be wise to take the ship out into the bay and ride out the storm free of the land. With a snort of annoyance, he dismissed the thought. This was no time for an experienced master mariner to be losing his nerve.

He began to pace up and down, his thoughts turning to the girl in the next room. Maybe he should have taken up her offer. He still could. She was an attractive little thing and *so what* if she had been aboard the trawler. Nearly two years of celibacy was a heavy burden for a man to carry. A distant flash of lightning lit up the darkening sky, cutting short the erotic fantasy his mind was about to weave. He took a mental cold shower. The whole thing was absurd. Two women had already made a mess of his life. Involvement with a third, even on a purely sexual basis, was the last thing he needed.

'Captain . . . Please . . .'

Powell swung round, his nerve ends jangling. Most of his drink spilled on the carpet. 'I thought I told you,' he began roughly, then his voice trailed off. Barefoot, her small figure swamped by his old silk dressing gown, she resembled nothing more threatening than a sleepy-eyed child pleading for postponement of her bedtime. She might easily have been his own daughter, as he had so often seen her in her days of innocence. Then, she moved towards him and the the mature sway of her hips cancelled out the child-like image.

Sweat broke out on his forehead. Brushing roughly past her, he reached down a second glass and poured two drinks, watching her out of the corner of his eye. The smell of fish was all around her and it no longer seemed unpleasant but sharp, spicy, exciting. His mind toyed with the picture of beer-swilling, red-faced trawlermen pawing her young body with salt-roughened hands. Somehow it didn't fit. It could be she was just an innocent girl down on her luck. A hippie? A runaway? His own daughter, Catrin, might well end up in the same circumstances.

He felt the need to make some form of apology as he handed her the glass. 'Drink it,' he said softly.

She took the glass without a word and drank deeply. The dark spirit might have been pure spring water for all the effect it had on her.

Powell winced. He had forgotten that many of her generation were hard drinkers from the cradle. 'Sit down,' he said.

She sat, holding her drink in her lap, her head bowed.

He faced her. 'Just what are you doing here?' he asked, not unkindly.

Without raising her eyes, she said in a small voice, 'There is a storm coming.' As if to add weight to her statement, the ship trembled as the rising wind rammed her against the jetty. Rain hammered on the thick glass of the potholes.

Powell found his patience flagging. 'I know there is a storm coming,' he said shortly. 'And I want you ashore before it comes. Do you understand that?'

A brilliant flash of lightning lit up the cabin, followed by the muted, ominous roll of thunder. The girl gave a low, agonised moan and threw herself at Powell, clasping herself close to him. 'Don't send me out into the storm,' she pleaded, her voice muffled by his shoulder. 'Please don't send me out there!'

He held himself tense, acutely conscious of the soft contours of her young body, inhaling the clean, salty perfume of her hair. She cried with great convulsive sobs, her tears soaking through the thin fabric of his shirt. Helpless in the face of such absolute fear, he put his arms around her and awkwardly kissed the top of her head. The lightning flared again and she burrowed closer to him, seeking sanctuary. 'It's all right,' he whispered. 'You can stay—until the storm is over, anyway . . .'

She looked up at him, the cold greyness of her eyes softened by tears. Her arms reached up encircling his neck and, pulling his head down, she kissed him full on the lips. He tasted salt and his nostrils flared, breathing deep the ozone-laden scent of her body, his own limbs stirring to a long forgotten passion. Fighting hard for control, he broke away. 'The storm will last all night,' he said huskily. 'You take my bed and I'll manage in the armchair.'

The girl gave him a puzzled look then, with a lopsided smile, she turned from him and padded towards the bedroom. In the shadow of the doorway, she slipped free of the dressing gown and paused, her slight curving figure silhouetted in the dim glow of the cabin lights. She looked back and said in a whisper, 'I will repay you for your kindness.' Then she was gone, into the darkness.

Powell smiled to himself. Nice thought. But there would be no repayment *her* way. Taking the half-empty bottle, he switched off the lights and settled himself in the scuffed leather armchair, an old friend of the long nights. He was loosening his tie when the internal phone rang.

'Your wife's on the outside phone, sir.' It was Baird.

Powell swore softly. He had nothing to say to Bethan. 'Tell her I'm not on board,' he grunted into the phone.

'She says it's about your daughter. Trouble I think.'

He reached the bridge in seconds and snatched up the ship to shore phone. 'Well?' he asked coldly.

'Huw?' Her voice was taut with anxiety.

'Who else would it be?' Powell answered testily. 'If you've got something important to say, Bethan, say it quickly. I'm on my way to bed.'

For a long moment, he could hear nothing but her tight breathing at the other end of the line. He began to hate himself. Perhaps she *really* needed help. Then, when she spoke, all the old bitterness gushed out. 'You selfish bastard, Huw Powell!' she breathed. 'You haven't changed a bit, have you?' He was about to slam the phone down when she went on. 'In case you're interested, your daughter's missing.'

'Missing?'

'Yes. Gone. Run away.'

Powell found himself gripping the handset tightly. 'Where? When did she go?' The attempt to sound casual fell flat.

'She left the house a week ago. She hasn't been back since. She's not staying with any of her friends.' Bethan's voice softened. 'This is serious, Huw.'

Powell hesitated. How many times in the past had Catrin flown the nest only to re-appear a few days later when her money had run out or her latest boyfriend had lost interest? All right . . . a week was a long time. The girl could be in trouble. He steeled himself. He was no longer part of this family. Why should he concern himself. 'What do you want *me* to do?' He asked, without a trace of emotion in his voice.

Again the silence. Then Bethan's voice, a little more than a whisper, 'She *is* your daughter.'

'*Was*,' he corrected and replaced the phone.

Returning to his cabin and the solitude of his armchair, he sat drinking, listening to the muted protests of his ship as the wind pushed and tugged at her moorings. Was he being too hard he asked himself. He was still married to Bethan and Catrin was his child. No matter which way you looked at it, he had a certain responsibility to bear. Then he remembered all the times in the past when his kindness had turned to softness and it had all been thrown back in his face. Giving in to everyone was a nice way to go through life but the rewards were always short-term. No. Bethan and Catrin had chosen their own life, completely excluding him. In that case, they must also face up to their problems without his help.

He poured himself another drink and sank back into the soft recesses of the armchair, his mind a tortured maelstrom. Was there nothing to be salvaged from twenty-two years of marriage? Did he really want the final and irrevocable separation? Did Bethan? In spite of the open antagonism they were showing towards each other, deep down there was still something pulling. There had never been any suspicion of another man in Bethan's life; not now or over the years. As for himself, although he sorely missed the company of women, both in bed and out, he had also kept clear of involvement; not out of any misplaced sense of purity but simply because the sordidness of the one night stand repelled him. Until tonight, perhaps? The urgent thrust of the girl's body against him still lingered. He chuckled drowsily. What if Bethan were to walk aboard now, eh? A naked girl in his bed; a girl young enough to be his daughter. Irrespective of whether the girl was a dockside tart on her rounds or a teenager out for kicks, Bethan would see it as a clear case of a dirty old man corrupting the innocent. She would loathe him. Blast the girl and her 'frightened of the storm' act! Blast her and her beautiful, silk-skinned body.

Powell stirred uneasily. He was avoiding the real issue. Catrin was gone and Bethan enough concerned about her absence to break a silence that had lasted half a year. Where could Catrin be? Gone off with some long-haired hippie, most likely. Travelling the countryside and sleeping rough like some penniless tramp. Or was she in trouble? Lying in some filthy hovel, bemused by drugs, being pawed about . . . He took a grip on his thoughts. He was confusing his daughter with the pathetic, young thing in the bed a bulkhead away from him. Catrin was hard. She could look after herself. He was worrying too much. The soothing fingers of the rum, aided by the gentle rocking of the ship, lulled him into a deep sleep.

At sometime during the night, he came awake with a start. The air was full of the angry crash of thunder. Lightning sizzled and flashed outside the ports, bathing the cabin in a blue, incandescent light. For several minutes he sat unmoving. The electric storm held no fears for him. Then he became aware of the alien sound which must have pulled him from his alcohol-assisted sleep. It was a low keening, which rose to a pitch of frenzy with each successive flash of lightning. Alarmed, he heaved himself to his feet and headed for the bedroom.

The girl, her bare skin shining in the eerie light, was curled up on the bed in a tight ball, like a small, defenceless animal seeking to escape the attack of a predator. Through the golden curtain of her hair, Powell could see her thin shoulders shaking with terror.

He bent over and put a comforting hand on her arm. With a grateful whimper, she rolled off the bed and clung to him. He held her close, as a father shelters a terrified child. But this was no child, he realised, as he fought to deny the soft pressure of her breasts, nipples tumescent, and the slow, challenging movement of her hips against his own. His resistance was brief and feeble. With a whispered curse, he pushed her back onto the bed. She watched, smiling and unembarrassed, as he feverishly threw off his clothes.

In the morning she was gone, leaving only an impression in his pillow and the taste of salt on his lips.

Slipping a towel around his waist, Powell went on deck and lounged contentedly against the ship's rail. The calm, pewter-tinted waters of the harbour winked back at him the rays of a weak sun shining out of a sky scoured clean by the night's storm. The girl had left him with a peace he had not known for many years. For a while, he stood filling his lungs with the cold, new air then, as he made to go inside, he caught sight of his old dressing gown draped over the rail. He laughed out loud. She had gone as she had apparently come— naked and unashamed. Back to her friends on the trawler, most likely.

He spent much of the morning in Ben Williams' office, discussing the more mundane aspects of ship operation; stores, bunkers, repairs. Shortly after eleven, when they had just decided to retire to the *Mariners Arms*, Powell was called to the phone.

It was Bethan again. His newly acquired peace of mind faded and he was tempted to hang up but there was a note of urgency in his wife's voice. 'What is it this time?' he said brutally, hating himself.

The antagonism was not returned. 'Huw,' Bethan said quietly. 'It's Catrin . . .' Her voice broke and he caught the sound of a muffled sob, Then, it all came out in an anguished flood. 'Oh, God . . . she tried to commit suicide, Huw. She tried to drown herself. Huw, what can I do? I know it's all my fault but . . .'

He cut her short. 'Forget the recriminations, Bethan. Is she all right?'

Bethan had regained her self-control but her voice still quavered. 'Yes . . . she's out of danger. In the Cottage Hospital. But I think you should be here, Huw. She needs her father. She needs us both. Do you understand, Huw?'

'Pencwm—as fast as you like!' Powell roared at a startled Ben Williams as he bundled him out of the office and into Ben's ancient Jaguar. They tore through the deserted country lanes, horn blaring, as though all the fiends of Hell were on their heels. The ten miles to Pencwm was covered in as many minutes.

Bethan was waiting for them at the gates of the small, weathered stone hospital. A forlorn figure but slim and eye-catching in a smart, dark blue jacket and skirt. She could have been a young thirty, except for the grey showing in her short, auburn hair and the deepening lines around her eyes. Those eyes, Powell saw, were reddened by tears. A wave of pity surged through him.

'I'll wait in the car,' Ben Williams said tactfully, as Powell tumbled out and half-ran towards his wife.

Awkwardly, Powell took Bethan's hand and bent to kiss her cheek. A small tremor of understanding passed between them as they touched. No words were spoken.

Bethan held onto his hand, clasping it tightly as they hurried along the clean-smelling flagstoned corridor. Outside the glass-panelled entrance to the wards, she stopped and turned to him. 'We almost lost her, Huw,' she said in a voice vibrant with anxiety. 'She was pulled out of the water half-drowned. It was no accident, she deliberately walked into the sea.' Her voice rose and tears welled into her eyes. 'She didn't want to live, Huw. We failed her, didn't we? Our stupid, petty quarrels almost drove our own daughter to suicide. If it hadn't been for the other girl . . .'

Powell gripped her arm. 'What other girl?'

Bethan winced and drew away from him. 'I don't know her name. She pulled Catrin out of the water and then ran away. They couldn't find her . . .'

'Come on,' Powell said brusquely, taking her arm again. 'All that can wait.'

When they were ushered into the single-bed ward, Catrin was propped up in bed, her face pale and drawn but, otherwise, she looked none the worse for her traumatic experience. Powell silently thanked a long forgotten God.

Catching sight of her mother, Catrin's eyes brightened then, as her father came into view, she averted her head quickly. Feeling the rebuff deeply, Powell sat on the edge of the bed and took the girl's unwilling hand in his. There was a boulder sized lump in his throat. 'Why, Catrin?' he asked softly, dreading the answer.

At first, she strained to pull away from him then, with an anguished cry, she turned and buried her head in his shoulder and began to cry with great, heart-rending sobs. Powell folded his arms around her and reflected guiltily that, for the second time in twenty-four hours, he was comforting a lonely, frightened girl-child. Across the bed, Bethan gave him a small, tremulous smile, a message of hope in her tear-filled eyes. He smiled back, wondering if they could make a new start.

Later in the day, Powell was able to get the full story from the local Coastguard. Shortly after dawn, while Powell lay in his rumpled bed with the smell of sex still heavy upon him, Catrin had walked, fully clothed into the icy waters of

Gwaun Bay and begun swimming out to sea. An early walker, exercising his dog on the beach, had reached the water's edge in time to see Catrin, now two hundred yards off-shore, disappear beneath the waves. Of what happened next, the man was confused but he spoke of another girl suddenly sur-facing with Catrin held in her arms. The girl then swam shorewards and landed her burden on the beach some dis-tance away. The man was elderly and, by the time he reached the spot, Catrin was face down in the sand coughing the sea out of her lungs and her unknown rescuer had vanished. As to where she had gone to, the man was vague; he thought back into the sea. But his description of her was precise. The girl was young, naked and had long, pale-brown hair that hung to her waist.

'I'd say the old man was not only confused but short-sighted, too,' Ben Williams remarked, when he and Powell were leaning on the bar of the *Mariners Arms* that evening. He gave a cynical laugh. 'Swimming in the nude at this time of the year, be damned! Next thing you know the old bloke'll be saying it was the famous Porthgwaun Mermaid.'

'It *was* the Mermaid,' the landlord announced in hushed tones. 'She was seen out in the bay last night.'

'Bullshit!' Ben Williams said into the bottom of his glass.

Powell was in a more receptive mood. 'Tell me about the Mermaid,' he asked.

The landlord shuffled uncomfortably. 'The story goes back a thousand years, Cap'n. There was a terrible storm on that night, see. Terrible nor'wester with the thunder crashing, the lightning sizzling and the rain streaming down like it did when Noah took to the Ark.' He paused to wipe the bar top with his cloth. 'There was Vikings around in those days,' he said, polishing the same spot nervously and keeping his head down. 'Bloody barbarians they were too. Going around raping and killing. Well . . . one of their ships took shelter in Gwaun Bay that night and, with the lightning flashing so that it was almost like day, they saw a beautiful mermaid resting on Black Rock. They caught this poor, innocent creature and tortured her something terrible before they killed her.'

Pausing to refill their glasses without invitation, the land-lord continued. 'Now, whenever there's a bad storm about—especially with thunder and lightning—the ghost of the Mermaid swims ashore and changes into a girl so that she can find the protection of a good man. It is said that the man who gives her shelter from the storm will be given a reward that is beyond value in this world.'

Powell's glass fell to the carpeted floor with a thud.

Ben Williams put out a hand to steady him. 'What's up, Huw? You look as though you've seen a ghost.'

'I may have, Ben,' Powell answered shakily. 'I may have done just that.'

SAILOR'S RETURN

It was late August 1943 when they brought my Dad home. A warm summer's evening with tiny, cotton wool clouds floating over Briog Head. Abernewydd Bay was blue enamel. Not even a catspaw of wind disturbed its slumbering peace. This was a summer for memories to be made—and they were.

Abernewydd station had never seen such crowds since Mr. Gwynfor Thomas, MP, opened this important terminus of the Great Western Railway in my great-grandfather's day. The official welcoming committee was made up of Mr. William John, Chairman of the Urban District Council, my Mam weeping great tears of pride and me, stiff and self-conscious in my Sunday suit; two sizes too big to allow for growing.

As the train pulled in the town band, out of tune but bursting with patriotism, launched into a rousing 'Men of Harlech.' At the same time, an elderly contingent of the local Home Guard, conveniently drawn up outside the Gents, shuffled to attention and presented arms with three twelve-bores, an air-rifle and five garden forks. *Diawch!* I was proud to be Welsh on that day.

My Dad was a war hero, see. He had been, in the words of the Western Mail, 'Injured while gallantly defending his ship during an enemy air raid on Cardiff Docks.' There had been strong talk of a medal but nothing came of it. Not many medals going for merchant seamen, you see. In any case, knowing my Dad, I was taking the whole story with a big pinch of salt. All the same, I was worried stiff. The arrival of this train could play havoc with my young life.

It was my family's proud boast that there had been an Abernewydd Davies at sea since 1671, when Ianto Davies wandered across the English border in an alcoholic daze, ending up as cook/steward to that distinguished Welsh pirate Sir Henry Morgan. This was a tradition not to be easily broken.

124

After my Dad, about to be returned to the bosom of his family with God-knows-what disability, I was next in line to carry the Davies' banner at sea.

Now, the sea and I didn't hit it off at all. We shared a mutual hatred born of a trip across Cardigan Bay in a leaking dinghy being chased by a roaring north-westerly. Sea sickness is a terrible thing, fear is another. The two combined convinced me that the sea should be left to those half-witted enough to enjoy it—which is mainly the English.

When the train jerked to a halt, Mr. Morgan Griffiths, Stationmaster, gave the signal and the doors of the guard's van were thrown ceremoniously open to reveal, recumbent on a stretcher and flanked by two simpering, middle-aged Red Cross Ladies, my Dad, Captain Owain Davies, Merchant Navy.

The band moved into a mournful rendering of 'For Those in Peril on the Sea' and Mr. William John, hurriedly inserting his false teeth, stepped forward to deliver the address of welcome. Unfortunately, my Dad chose that moment to be sick all over the patent leather shoes of one of his attendants. My keen, young nostrils detected a distinct smell of Guinness. 'The Cap'n' had been well fortified on his long journey across the Principality.

Mr. William John abandoned his oration and stepped back muttering, 'Get the bugger on the cart before he ruins everything.'

While my Mam was wiping down the defiled Red Cross lady, who was emitting genteel twitters of disgust, the stretcher was manhandled onto the platform and placed reverently in Jones-the-Milk's handcart. The National Health Service still being some years off, there was no ambulance in Abernewydd.

At last, the procession was formed and we set off to cover the two miles to our house in Lower Town. More sensible it would have been to hire a lorry to run my Dad home but emotions were riding high that day. Much of this was due to Mr. William John who, having aspirations to become Lord Mayor of Cardigan, had decreed there would be 'a ceremony in keeping with the solemnity of the occasion.' And so we shuffled through the station gates led by the band playing the 'Dead March in Saul'. This, I thought, was carrying the solemnity business too far, especially as I could hear my Dad's voice above the muffled beat of the music shouting, 'Where's the bloody ale?'

Immediately behind Jones-the-Milk's handcart walked my Mam, looking very regal in best funeral-going hat. I followed on my bike, pedalling slow in time with the music. Then came the po-faced Mr. William John, Mr. Mog Evans—the-Post and the Reverend Ifor James—six foot two and smiling tipsily through his black beard. Behind them, an untidy crocodile of relations, friends and hangers-on, all attracted by the prospect of free beer and sandwiches when they reached our house.

As we thumped our way impressively along the beach road, my mind was in a fever of activity. I was almost seventeen years old and my call-up papers imminent. Not that I minded fighting for my country. At the very least, it would get me away from the stifling atmosphere of Abernewydd County School. But, if I had to die young, I reasoned, how much better it would be to die attacking the enemy—at the controls of a Spitfire, perhaps? Yes . . . I would fight *my* war in the sky. Bugger the Davies press gang and the sea.

It was a long pull up the hill overlooking the bay. The band flagged at its sonorous beat. The Sea Scouts, who had been given the honour of propelling the hero's carriage, could do no more than inch it up the steep gradient. The whole grumbling procession became dustier and sweatier with every yard covered. Some began to question the wisdom of their enthusiasm. The only one to take it all in his stride—metaphorically speaking, of course—was Cap'n Owain Davies. Throughout, he lay back with a blissful smile on his face. The two flagons of ale placed in the cart by a well-wisher, were now empty. Seeing these caused me to give thought to the terrible thirst I was working up myself.

Breasting the top of the hill, I rode on ahead, tongue hanging out at the prospect of a sly half-pint at the side door of the Royal Oak. My haste to be first at the trough proved to be a mistake. Passing the County School, I almost ran over

Maggie John. The only daughter of Mr. William John, Maggie was one of the many crosses I had to bear at that stage of my young life.

'And where do you think you're going in such a hurry, David Davies?' Miss John called in her toffee-nosed English voice. Her father being an important man in the town, she felt obliged to act like royalty sometimes. Sorry I was I ever put my hand up her skirt that night in the back seat of the pictures. Since then, she had acted as though she owned me. Always clinging to my arm and dawdling in front of Harries Bros., Quality Furnishers.

A soft touch I was for women, even in those days. No sooner was I off my bike than Maggie had me in the school air raid shelter professing my undying love and struggling to get inside the long school mack she wore tightly buttoned summer and winter.

Half an hour later, my passion cooled by Maggie's knee in my groin, we got back on the road to find it deserted, except for Old Man Monti pedalling his ice cream cart like mad in the direction of the Square. No sign or sound of the procession but I didn't need two guesses at where they would be. Perching Maggie on the crossbar of my bike, I set off in pursuit.

We went down High Street like a rocket, with Maggie giving a shocking, but not unwilling display of brown lisle stockings. When we passed Old Man Monti, he became so excited that he rode his cart straight into the plate glass window of Jones Bros., High Class Butcher.

Abernewydd Square was as empty as the beach on a wet Sunday. The same could not be said for the Royal Oak. The brass instruments of the band were lined up outside like a row of guardsmen and the noise coming from the saloon bar was deafening. Telling Maggie to watch the bike—there being some thieving gentlemen in Abernewydd—I slid around the side door.

I peered into the saloon bar. 'Cwm Rhondda' they were on, 'Myfanwy' it would be next, with them all crying in their beer and reciting the past glories of Wales. Mr. William John, Mr. Mog Evans and the Reverend Ifor James were shoulder to shoulder and sinking pints as fast as Dilys Evans, the bar-maid could pull them. There was no sign of my Dad.

'Where's my Dad, Dilys?' I asked, when she found time to slip across with a brimming half-pint under her apron. Lovely big woman, Dilys was, and she fancied me. Disgusting really. She was nearly old enough to be my mother. Well . . . at least thirty.

'Now, don't you worry, David *bach*,' Dilys purred. 'The Cap'n's gone on ahead with your Mam. I expect they want to be private for a bit, him being away so long,' she added with a lewd wink. She came close, bringing a waft of her perfume. Cheap scent it was, with a dash of sweat and stale beer. I tried to back off but her arm was around me, squashing me to her comfortable bosom. 'There's a brave man your Dad is,' she cooed. 'They do say the English will give him a medal. Aren't you proud, *cariad*?'

Proud I should have been but worried I was. The warm, softness of Dilys and the half-pint I'd downed in one gulp were turning my knees to water. But my head was as clear as a bell and that bell was clanging out a warning. My Dad had the knack of making the best of any situation and I could see him using this one as a stepping stone to a quiet and perman-ent life ashore. No two guesses at who would have to take his place at sea.

Maggie was in a terrible huff when I came back outside. Hated Dilys Evans, she did. 'I suppose you've been making up to that old woman again,' she said cattily. I bundled her back onto the crossbar without a word. I had had enough of the moods of women for one day.

We set off through the empty town, me holding my head to one side to keep the beer fumes from Maggie's twitching nos-trils. I needn't have bothered. She was lecturing me on the evils of drink before we reached the top of the hill. I have never been able to understand why that the two greatest pleasures in a man's life, women and drink, must for ever be at war with each other.

Terrible is the hill down from Abernewydd to Lower Town. One in eight and as tortuous as the path of a paralytic snake. Half way down, I could see the tattered remains of my father's triumphal procession. The Royal Oak had taken its toll. The few faithful who remained were either too young to drink or, like my Mam, very chapel and strict teetotal.

Unmoved by the desertion of so many of his followers, my Dad lay sleeping blissfully, an empty flagon clasped to his chest. But, as I drew close, disaster struck. The tiny figures of the Sea Scouts lost their struggle to hold the cart on the near-vertical slope and were scattered like so much chaff in the wind. Jones-the-Milk's handcart trundled off down the hill, gathering speed as it went.

I didn't give much for my Dad's chances of survival. There was a right-angled bend at the foot of the hill, which he had no earthly hope of negotiating. Straight into the harbour he would go, with the cart on top of him. Unless I did something very quickly, the tide being in and my Dad a non-swimmer, I was about to be condemned to a long and painful career at sea.

Skidding to a halt alongside my Mam, who was having hysterics, I disembarked Maggie and raced on down the hill in pursuit of my salvation. My brakes failed when I reached the bend and I sailed horror-stricken into the muddy waters of the harbour.

Fighting my way clear of the tangled remains of my bike, I surfaced and trod water as I looked around. Nothing in sight. No wreckage, not even a string of bubbles to show my Dad was lurking on the bottom deliberately filling his lungs with water. He was quite capable of pulling a trick like that.

With my best suit having soaked up half the Atlantic Ocean and threatening to drag me under, I floundered ashore and crawled up over the sea wall. I squelched across the harbour bridge, dreading what I might find the other side. Here, the road ran straight at a row of stone-built cottages before veering sharply to the left. But there was no splintered wreckage, no gory mess on someone's front doorstep.

Around the corner and fifty yards up the road, Jones-the-Milk's handcart was parked unscathed outside the Ship Inn. For my Dad, I knew I would have to look no further.

Spotting an open window in the bar, I sidled wetly up to it. God and Owain Davies must have been on good terms that

day. Totally unmarked by his headlong descent into Lower
Town, pint in hand and surrounded by his cronies, my Dad
was holding court.

'Tell us about Cardiff, Owain,' a voice urged as I listened.

'Did those bloody Germans machine gun you when you
was in the water?' asked another.

'Is it true they will give you a medal?' This from the landlord.

As I watched, my father's face went deep red with embarrassment. 'Now, hang on, boys!' he burst out. 'All this talk
about medals have gone far enough.' He gave a worried glance
around the tiny, smoke-filled room. 'I'll give you the truth,
boys. But not a word outside these four walls, right?'

There was a grunted chorus of 'Not a word, Cap'n.'

'It was like this, see,' my Dad went on. 'Me and the chief
engineer had slipped ashore in Cardiff for a quiet pint one
night—awful strain on a man this old war is. Well . . . we was
coming out of this boozer in Mountstuart Square when the
sirens went.' He paused to take a long pull at his beer, then
continued. 'Of course, us being good, loyal Welsh seamen
and knowing where our duty lay, we rushed across the road
to get back through the dock gates. Now . . . what with the
sirens screaming, the guns banging and me with seven pints
of best bitter inside me, I did a daft thing. Ran right in front of
a tram, I did. Came to in the Royal Infirmary. Hurt my back
something awful I had, but they didn't reckon I would die.
Nothing much would have been said but a reporter from the
Western Mail buggered the whole thing up. Wrote a story
about me sticking to my ship all through the raid, even
though I was wounded.'

'There's brave you were, Owain,' the landlord breathed
reverently.

My Dad held up his hand, face red again. 'Brave, nothing! I
was drunk, mun. But the old Chief was drunker than me.
After the tram knocked me down, the silly sod carried me all
the way back to the ship and dumped me on board. Slept all
through the raid, I did . . .'

Crouched at the window, with the chill wind of evening
seeping through my wet clothes, I decided I had heard
enough. I went home to dry off and await developments.

It took just twenty-four hours for him to bring up the subject of the Davies maritime tradition. 'Those old Germans have really done for me, boy,' he whined, propped up in the big double bed with a hot water bottle at his back. 'You'll have to get yourself off to sea now, Davy. You know what the family's like . . .'

He went green when I told him I had no intention of taking his place at sea and even greener when I threatened to expose him, not only to my Mam but to the Council, which had just voted to make him a freeman of the town.

Very crafty my Dad was. Three weeks later, he went walking on Briog Head and never came back. 'Accidental death', the Coroner called it, although the body was never found. Funny that Dilys Evans disappeared at the same time. To this day, I swear they went off to live in sin together.

After my Dad's so-called death, the family closed ranks against me and, with Great-uncle Tom handling the negotiations, a cadetship was arranged for me with the Cambrian Steampacket Company of Cardiff. Within two months, I was afloat.

My first, and only, trip to sea was a cruel nightmare. Leaving Cardiff with a full cargo of coal for Freetown, we became the target of every U-boat in the North Atlantic. It was as though Hitler himself had decreed that I, David Davies, should not survive. All we had to fight back with was a 1918 4-inch that couldn't hit a barn door at ten yards.

The final ignominy came when we struck a mine in the entrance to Freetown harbour, blocking the channel and showering the local inhabitants with lumps of best Welsh coal.

That wasn't my idea of how to fight a war. As soon as my survivor's leave was up, I was hot-foot to Haverfordwest to join the RAF. Became a fighter pilot too, I did. But, by then, the war was over. The only thing I ever got a crack at was the summit of Snowdon. I ran full tilt into it when the cloud was low and my altimeter reading high. I can manage quite well in this wheelchair, though—except for that bloody right-angled bend at the bottom of the hill.

THE FINAL ROUND

The first day of May 1945 dawned full of promise. In Europe, the war was in its final stages, with the victorious armies of the Allies closing in on a rapidly disintegrating German Third Reich. Further east, the population of the Japanese islands, hitherto confident in the invincibility of their Emperor and their cause, were wavering uncertainly in the path of advancing retribution. The systematic destruction of mankind, so gloriously entered upon in 1939, was running out of steam.

Unperturbed by the petty bickerings of man, the South Indian Ocean basked calm and secure in the autumn sunshine. Two tiny pinpricks of irritation alone disturbed the otherwise unruffled surface of this great sea.

Fifteen hundred miles to the eastward of the African mainland, a pocket of warm, moisture-laden air approached the small island of Rodriquez. Here, the westerly precession of this unstable air was halted by the towering peak of Mount Limon and forced into a rapid ascent, losing even more stability as it rose. At 20,000 feet, the growing area of turbulence toppled and fell into an ominous, spiralling circulation. It then began to move westwards at an ever increasing pace, generating within itself the awesome, destructive forces of a tropical cyclone. Far below, the inhabitants of Rodriquez continued to eat, sleep and multiply, unaware of the monster spawned over their beautiful island.

Northwards, high in the Mozambique Channel, a second and more insidious source of irritation lurked. *U-316*, erstwhile razor-edged killing machine of Hitler's Kreigsmarine, now battered and rust-stained, lolled idly in the long, gentle swell. In her conning tower, which bore the ugly scars of recent depth charging, Kapitan-Lieutenant Willy Mueller peeled off his shirt and marvelled at the touch of the hot sun on his bare skin.

At 28, Mueller's corn-coloured hair was already showing grey, while his tall, wiry frame was stooped from countless hours of bending to the periscope's whim. For him it had been a long and punishing war. He leaned over the rim of the conning tower, surveying his crew romping naked and uncaring on the casing below, their putty-white bodies flushing pink in the rejuvenating warmth. He scratched slowly at his ragged beard. 'Enjoy yourselves while you can, you poor bastards,' he said half-aloud. 'There's not much time left for you now.'

Time had, in fact, been running out for *U-316* from the moment she cleared the Weser, three months earlier. From the very outset, she had been hunted like a high-priced game fish. The enemy, with the scent of victory widening his nostrils, had been relentless and vindictive. Running, darting, backtracking, *U-316* had blundered her way through the fog-shrouded North Passage out into the long swells of the Atlantic. Here, the chase had continued day after day, with the seemingly endless, slamming depth charges turning the cramped, sweating pressure hull into a living hell for Mueller and his men. Miraculously, contact had been lost in the broad reaches of the South Atlantic but, skirting the Cape of Good Hope, the insistent fingers of the enemy's asdic had once again sought them out. Only when a desperate Mueller had begun to draw his pursuers down towards the ice-edge of Antartica had the chase been grudgingly abandoned.

Despite the unrelenting harrassment by the enemy, Mueller, young in body but old in the ways of war, had made good use of the few opportunities presented to him. In his twisting wake 30,000 tons of Allied shipping lay scattered over the ocean bottoms.

Now Mueller was waiting patiently for what he knew would be his last kill. His remaining attacking power consisted of one single torpedo and six rounds for the deck gun. When they were gone, there would be no replenishment. Germany was a whole world away, the supply ships sunk and the once accommodating neutral ports turned suddenly hostile. It was unlikely that *U-316* would see Bremerhaven again so time was of little importance. Mueller was content to wait in the shadows. However long it took, he meant to finish his war with one last sitting duck, plump, succulent and defenceless preferred.

The South African port of Durban, accustomed in these wartime days to a forest of tall masts, swinging derricks and smoking funnels, was all but devoid of shipping. A few salt-caked whalers, a floating crane and a motley collection of retired trawlers did nothing to dispel the pathetic air of desertion. Only one vessel of any significance remained in the harbour, and the tugs were already fussing around her.

The steamship *Lady Priscilla* was the first-born in a long line of profitable general cargo carriers owned by Frinton, Howells and Frinton (Shipowners) of London. Of 6000 tons gross, 410 feet in length and 51 feet in the beam, the *Lady Priscilla* was a tired, elderly lady with rapidly deteriorating machinery. She had been named after the first wife of Sir Charles Frinton, senior partner, and had grown old in a life of hard and dedicated service to her owners. Her namesake had long since been put out to grass; Sir Charles having taken himself a younger and more nubile wife, with whom he was ecstatically copulating himself into an early grave. It was a matter for much speculation in shipping circles as to who would go first, Sir Charles or the *Lady Priscilla*. So long as the war lasted, the *Lady P* was safe from the knackers yard. Sir Charles, on the other hand, had no such assurance.

From his vantage point in the wing of the bridge, Captain James Walton viewed with dismay the confusion reigning on the deck below him. Hatchboards were being slammed into place with indecent haste, tarpaulins dragged across at the run and wedges thumped home with quick, desperate hammer blows. Lascar seamen, urged on by the strident shouts of the deck serang, scurried from hatch to hatch in a mounting frenzy. Concurrent with all this unseemly activity, the *Lady Priscilla* was being plucked unceremoniously from her berth by two powerful tugs belching steam and smoke as their propellors threshed astern.

James Walton, tall, angular, with a shock of pure white hair, was of the old school of shipmasters, a product of an age when the term 'shipshape and Bristol fashion' had a meaning. To proceed to sea with his ship not fully prepared to do battle with the elements meant to him the betrayal of a lifetime's training. Little wonder his normally ruddy face was now brick-red with frustration. However, on this occasion, he had little choice but to subdue his natural instincts. Due to slow delivery of cargo alongside the ship, indifferent African dockers and a last minute boiler repair, the *Lady Priscilla* was in danger of losing the protection of the convoy assembled and waiting outside the port. Any other time, the fiercely independent Walton would have told the convoy to go to hell and left port in his own good time. Unfortunately, that option was not now open to him. His cargo of army lorries, tanks and ammunition, sitting on a heavy bottom weight of bagged cement, needed the protection of the Royal Navy's guns.

★   ★   ★   ★

'Wind's freshening, sir!' Thomas Holbrook, the *Lady Priscilla*'s stocky, red-haired chief officer observed, as they cleared the twin breakwaters of Durban harbour.

Captain Walton steadied himself against the roll of the ship and nodded. The wind was in the south-east and increasing. Wisps of high cirrus cloud streaked an otherwise flawless blue sky. Danger signs. 'Could be something brewing out there, Mister Holbrook,' Walton said, indicating the horizon to the east. 'Best double up on the hatch battens. We don't want any water down below with this lot in us.'

With a breezy, 'I'll see to it right away, sir,' Holbrook clattered down the ladder, bound for the weather deck.

'Commodore's signalling, sir!' a pink-cheeked cadet called nervously from the flying bridge, where he kept earnest watch with a long, brass telescope. 'Convoy speed ten knots, sir,' he read out slowly.

'Acknowledge!' Walton flung back irritably. Ten knots, indeed! Pigs might fly.

The *Lady Priscilla* could, by no stretch of the imagination, be called an ocean flyer. Her triple-expansion, steam-reciprocating engine, fed by three coal-fired Scotch boilers, produced, when pushed, a maximum of 9½ knots. But it was pointless to argue with the power of the Admiralty. At the Commodore's conference, prior to sailing, Walton had cannily kept silent when the Commodore had announced in a no-nonsense voice, 'Convoy speed will be ten knots; and I want no stragglers, gentlemen. Is that understood?' In the absence of any protests from the assembled merchant ship masters, he had turned to a large chart of the South Atlantic pinned to the wall and traced his pointer along the inked-in courses. 'Our route will take us well south of Madagascar, passing about 100 miles east of Rodriquez, 150 miles east of Diego Garcia and then straight up to Bombay.' He looked around at the dozen, or so, expressionless faces. 'I know most of you gentlemen would prefer to take the shorter route up the Mozambique Channel but I'm not prepared to take that chance. Too damned easy for the odd Jerry sub to be holed up there waiting for us.'

Walton raised his binoculars and took a sweep around the convoy. It was not an inspiring sight. Fourteen merchant vessels, all general cargo carriers and loaded dangerously near to their marks with army supplies for the forthcoming assault on Japanese-held Burma. Most of the ships, like the *Lady Priscilla*, were ancient and vulnerable. They were armed, after a fashion, with a motley collection of vintage guns unlikely to be of any use against a professional adversary. Anxiously circling the convoy was its sole escort, a brace of wheezing destroyers, which might well have seen service with Beatty at Jutland.

'What do you think of our chances with this lot, Mister?' Walton asked his chief officer, who had rejoined him on the bridge.

Holbrook gave a wry grin and reached for his binoculars. 'I suppose it's better than being on our own, sir,' he said, focusing on one of the RN ships.

Is it? Walton thought. The so-called 'safe' route outside of Madagascar meant an extra three days steaming. Three more days in which they would be exposed to possible danger. A lone dash up the Mozambique Channel sounded a much better proposition.

The cyclone struck when the convoy was three days out of Durban and to the south-west of the great island of Madagascar. The swell came first; long, rolling hills of water, carrying their warning message hundreds of miles ahead of the eye of the storm. Overnight, the barometer fell at a frightening pace, bringing with it a southerly wind that strengthened with every millibar lost. By the time the first pale fingers of dawn were probing the eastern sky, the wind was force 11 and still rising. Huge waves, with long, overhanging crests came marching in, beam on to the convoy's course. Flying spray, torn from the tops of the waves, filled the air with a blinding, salt-laden whiteness. Within an hour after full daylight, the heavily loaded merchant ships were staggering drunkenly under the onslaught of wind and sea. A reduction of speed was signalled but, one by one, the ships were forced to heave-to head to wind, in order to ride out the giant rollers with minimal damage to themselves. What had once been organised convoy degenerated into a confused huddle of ships, each fighting its own individual duel with the elements.

The *Lady Priscilla*, her bottom weight of cement giving her a hideous, pendulum-like motion, was an early straggler and fighting a desperate, losing battle. Each time she was brought up into the wind, her tired old engine was unable to maintain steerage way for more than a few minutes and she relentlessly fell back into the trough to wallow helplessly, until her bows could be once more forced around. This agonising performance was repeated time and time again until, finally, the weary vessel fell headlong into a deep valley, beam on to a huge, white-topped mountain of water. Hidden amongst the howling turmoil of the storm, the freak wave had found her.

Red eyed, his face deep-lined with fatigue, Walton watched powerless as the towering sea, its angry crest curling over, rolled down on his ship.

'Christ! Just look at that bloody monster!' Holbrook, fear roughening his voice, shouted above the scream of the wind.

Walton offered no comment but stood, legs braced wide, hands gripping the wooden taffrail as he gauged the awesome power of the advancing sea. He had always had supreme confidence in his sturdy ship, but this was something far beyond the realms of her previous adversaries.

The huge wall of water crashed into the thick, steel plates of the *Lady Priscilla*'s starboard side with the force of a gigantic battering ram, pushing her bodily sideways and down into the depths of the trough. As the base of the wave slowed with the shock of the collision, the crest toppled and came roaring down on the defenceless ship.

All but blinded by the flying spray, Walton groaned in horror as the deck below him disappeared under thousands of tons of seething, green water. The *Lady Priscilla* lurched and, for a while, it seemed she was unable to rise from beneath the colossal weight pressing down on her. Then, she rolled sluggishly to port, shedding water over her bulwarks and through her clanging freeing ports. With agonising slowness, she heaved herself upright and the men watching white-faced on her bridge saw her streaming deck emerge from the depths.

Frustrated, the elements showed their teeth in ugly leer. Thunder cannonaded around the horizon, backgrounding brilliant forks of lightning, which sent angry fireballs sizzling off the surface of the sea. The black, hanging clouds shook their skirts spitefully, releasing great torrents of needle-sharp rain.

Walton jammed his cap low over his eyes, straining to assess the damage on deck. Although he could see no further than the cargo hatch immediately below the bridge, he knew his ship had suffered a grievous blow. In plain sight were two heavy steel derricks, still suspended from the mast by their wire topping lifts but wrenched from their restraining crutches and swinging crazily across the hatch, carving a swathe of destruction in their wake. The two liferafts forward of the bridge had already gone, to be quickly followed by one, two, three galvanized steel ventilator cowls, shorn off by the rampaging derricks leaving gaping holes in the deck two feet across. Worse was to come. As Walton watched, a rush of water came down the deck carrying with it the splintered remains of several wooden hatchboards. It was clear that one of the forward hatches had been breached by the sea.

Swinging around, Walton bundled his chief officer into the shelter of the wheelhouse. Once inside, with the demoniacal shriek of the wind barely muted, he bellowed into the other man's ear. 'One of the for'ard hatches has gone! Smashed in! I'm going to put her stern on and make a run for it up the Mozambique Channel. To hell with the convoy!'

★　　★　　★　　★

Leutnant-zur-See Horst Dreyfus made a small, precise cross on the chart. 'We are here, Kapitan,' he said. 'Exactly forty miles due west of the island of Juan de Nova.'

Kapitan-Leutnant Mueller picked up the dividers and leaned over to study the chart closely. He stepped off the distance from the pencilled position to the mainland of Africa. It matched the distance to Juan de Nova to a mile.

Mueller nodded. 'Well done, Horst. That puts us right in the middle of the Mozambique Channel. We couldn't be better placed.' He straightened up with a laugh. 'Just like the cork in the neck of a bottle, eh Horst?'

The fresh-faced first lieutenant grinned nervously. 'If any Tommy ships come up this way, they're in for a shock. We can't miss them, sir.'

Mueller lit one of his favourite black cheroots and puffed thoughtfully. 'They'll come all right, Horst. But we'll have to work damned hard for anything we get. Eighty miles is a lot of ocean for one boat to guard. The convoys usually go to the east of Madagascar, remember, so if anything comes up this channel, it's likely to be one ship making a run on its own. She'll be difficult to spot and,' he added grimly, 'unless she's a sitting duck, the devil's own job to sink with only one torpedo and half a dozen shells left.'

Dreyfus returned to the chart. 'A continuous sweep between Juan de Nova and the mainland, sir?'

'Exactly, Leutnant! A day and night patrol on the surface. East to west and west to east. Lookouts doubled and every man on his toes.' Mueller hammered on the chart table with his fist, scattering the instruments. 'If a Tommy comes this way, I mean to have him! Now, set the watches and get under way.'

★   ★   ★   ★

Under a cloudless, blue sky, the *Lady Priscilla* headed north at a comfortable eight knots, her blunt bows nudging aside a glassy calm sea. Captain James Walton, cool and crisp in his freshly laundered, white uniform, swept the horizon ahead with his binoculars. 'Yachting weather this, Mister Holbrook, eh?' he said, without interrupting his survey.

Tom Holbrook removed his cap and wiped the sweat from his forehead with the back of his hand. 'All very nice, Captain,' he grunted. 'But it's too bloody clear for my liking. Jerry'll be able to spot us twenty miles off.'

Walton lowered his glasses and smiled. 'We can't have it all ways, Tom. Forty-eight hours ago, we would have given our souls for weather like this.' He paused to put a match to his pipe, sending out clouds of blue-grey smoke that hung in the still air. 'In any case,' he went on, 'I don't think we're likely to run into trouble now. As far as the Germans are concerned, the war's over and I don't see any Japs coming this far west.'

Holbrook sucked his teeth thoughtfully. 'All the same, sir . . . I'll be damned glad when we get clear of this channel. Gives me the creeps, this place. Too quiet by far.'

'You *are* a bloody pessimist,' Walton said with a chuckle. 'I could do with some good news for a change. How about the repairs on deck? Everything squared up?'

'I've done what I can, sir. Number two hatch is secure and I've put plugs and covers on the ventilators we lost.' Holbrook shook his head. 'Nothing much I can do about the derricks at Number Three. Have to get the shore squad onto them in Bombay.'

Walton nodded. 'Good work, Tom. Anything else?'

Holbrook glanced nervously up at the tall funnel soaring 60 feet above the bridge. 'I don't feel too happy about that funnel. Two of the stays parted in the cyclone and the whole thing must have been on the move. I've found a nasty crack in the base.'

Unworried, Walton resumed his search of the horizon. 'Rig some extra stays, then. It'll last until we get to Bombay.'

As Holbrook murmured agreement and turned to go, the Captain called after him, 'And tell the 2nd Mate to exercise the crew on the 4-inch this morning! Just as well to be prepared . . .'

★   ★   ★   ★

The sun reluctantly detached its lower limb from the horizon and began its curving ascent to the zenith. In the cramped conning tower of *U-316*, Leutnant-zur-See Horst Dreyfus shrugged off his heavy watch coat, welcoming the first warmth of the day. Even though, the submarine's line of patrol was only 17 degrees south of the Equator, the nights were chilly.

A waft of cigar smoke coming from the conning tower hatch announced the arrival of Kapitan Mueller, freshly shaved and breakfasted. 'Perfect weather, Horst. It could almost be the Alster in June, eh?' he said cheerfully, looking around at the unblemished sea and sky as he squeezed in alongside the 1st Lieutenant.

Dreyfus came to attention and touched his cap in salute, his nostrils twitching in anticipation as he savoured the salami, rye bread and real coffee waiting for him below. 'A fine morning, sir,' he acknowledged. 'But not a thing in sight yet.'

Mueller waved his cheroot expansively. 'We've got plenty of time, Horst. Fresh water may become a problem, but not yet.' He bent over to check the compass repeater. 'Right . . . you go below and get something to eat. I'll take over for a while.'

Alone in the conning tower, Mueller ran his eye over his command. She was a sad sight, he concluded. Her casing was pockmarked with shell holes and buckled by depth charges in a dozen places. But these were proud scars. Scars received in so many skirmishes with a vastly superior enemy. Had it all been worth the effort? he thought. So many men had died in the last three wearying months, fighting a war that was already lost. Germany was finished, her armies humbled, her cities in ruins. He focused his Zeis 10 x 50's and made a slow, searching sweep around the horizon. It was as barren as it had been for the last, despairing five days. Not even a bird or a porpoise disturbed the monotonous blue acres of sea and sky.

Mueller cursed aloud. Where was his plump, sitting duck? How much longer would he have to wait? He was determined to strike one more blow for Germany before the end came—and, despite his outward show of confidence, he knew that for *U-316* the end was very near. Fuel was running dangerously low, the boat's fighting capability pitifully limited. The opportunity would need to present itself very soon and, when it came—if it came—the attack would have to be fast and accurate. With only one torpedo and six rounds for the 105mm gun remaining, there would be no second chance.

James Walton paced the bridge of his ship with growing apprehension. He was now nearing the most crucial point in his lone passage. Abeam to starboard, and below his visible horizon, lay the remote island of Juan de Nova. To port, and also out of sight, sweltered the mangrove-fringed shores of Portuguese East Africa. This narrowest of bottlenecks in the Indian Ocean had, for years, been the favoured killing ground of Germany's long range submarines. If the attack was to come, it would surely be here in these restricted waters. Walton turned his anxious thoughts to the deadly mixture of cargo in the *Lady Priscilla*'s holds. One torpedo would be enough. Her hull would be ripped apart by the instantaneous detonation of the 800 tons of bombs, shells and mines she carried. The shattered remains would be dragged gurgling to the ocean bed by the sheer, compact weight of the 4000 tons of cement. Whichever way you looked at it, the prospect was frightening. Walton could see only one faint hope of survival. Speed was the answer. The faster he took his ship out of this hazardous area, the more chance there would be of reaching Bombay.

His mind made up, Walton gave the orders. 'Mister Holbrook! Call the engineroom. Tell the Chief to screw the safety valves down. I want every revolution he can give me for the next twelve hours. No arguments, tell him! Full emergency speed!'

The *Lady Priscilla*'s Lascar firemen quickened the swing of their shovels as they fed coal to the nine hungry furnaces of the huge Scotch boilers. The steam pressure mounted slowly and the beat of the three great reciprocating pistons gathered pace. Crockery in the officers saloon rattled excitedly, the magnetic compass danced crazily in its gimbals and a long plume of black, sulphurous smoke poured from the mouth of the funnel ninety feet above sea level.

'Smoke bearing red four-oh!' Willy Mueller had his glasses on the bearing before the lookout had finished calling out. It was smoke all right; a thin, black pencil climbing out of the distant horizon on the port bow. As Mueller watched, the excitement mounting within him, the smoke was joined by the tips of two masts, elongated by the horizon haze. His hand hit the alarm button, sending the urgent screech of the klaxon resounding throughout the boat. Their faces tense, the hardened veterans of *U-316* moved swiftly to their battle stations. Signallers and machine gunners crowded into the conning tower, while the five-man crew of the 105mm deck gun tumbled out of the forward hatch, clearing and loading their weapons with faultless precision. In thirty-five seconds, Leutnant Dreyfus was able to report, 'All closed up, sir!'

Mueller handed his binoculars to Dreyfus. 'Take a look, Horst.'

Dreyfus focussed the glasses to his own eyes and studied the approaching ship. A tall, unraked funnel and the square, unmistakeable superstructure of a large merchant ship were now visible. '*Gott verdammt*, Kapitan!' he breathed. 'A big, fat one.'

Mueller chuckled. 'The sitting duck, Horst. Heading north on her own, if I'm not mistaken.' He retrieved his binoculars and gestured towards the voicepipe. 'Bring her round on an interception course and group up both engines for maximum revolutions. We'll get as close as possible before we submerge for the attack. Time now?'

The 1st lieutenant glanced at his watch. 'O945, sir.'

'Right! Prepare to dive in exactly fifteen minutes—at 1000 hours.'

Captain Walton re-appeared on the bridge of the *Lady Priscilla*, having snatched a late breakfast in his cabin. The sun was now high in the sky and beating down with tropical fierceness. No cloud marred the sky, except the long pall of smoke streching back from the *Lady Priscilla*'s funnel.

Walton took out his pipe and started to ream the bowl with his clasp knife. 'Can't you get the engineers to do something about that bloody smoke?' he grumbled. 'They'll be able to see us on the other side of Madagascar.'

Tom Holbrook shrugged helplessly. 'I've told them a dozen times but they say there's damn all they can do about it at this speed. The old Chief's having a fit down there.'

Walton blew down his pipe. 'As long as he keeps the thing going, he's entitled to have a fit,' he said with a smile. He looked around at the flawless seascape and then up at the plume of smoke and his smile faded. 'I suppose we'll have to live with it until it gets dark. What wouldn't I give for a good North Sea fog, right now.'

Holbrook looked back at the trailing column of smoke and pursed his lips. 'We could try a zig-zag, sir,' he said cautiously.

'Yes . . . I've been considering that,' Walton said, clasping the empty pipe between his teeth. 'Might not be a bad idea—until sunset, at least. What speed is she doing now?'

'Nearly twelve knots, sir.'

Walton whistled. 'No wonder the Chief's worried.' He nodded towards the chartroom. 'Get the convoy book out, Tom, and look up a simple zig-zag. We'll lose a good knot on it but it may give us a better chance if there are any U-boats around.' He glanced at his watch. 'Start the zig-zag in half an hour from now . . . at 10.30.'

'Slow ahead together. Up periscope!' Mueller crouched low and caught the handles of the periscope as it slid out of the well with a quiet hiss. When the lens broke the surface, he swung through a precautionary 360 degrees before focussing on the approaching target. She was alone, the Red Ensign flapping defiantly at her stern clearly visible. 'British merchant, ship', Mueller called out for the benefit of the others in the control room. 'About 6000 tons and fully loaded. Steady on a northerly course.'

'Number One tube loaded, sir!' Dreyfus answered, a nervous tremor in his voice.

Mueller gripped the handles of the periscope and smiled grimly. Number One tube it had to be. The others were as empty as a Friesian farmer's purse. Sweat broke out on his forehead as he centred the crosswires on the unsuspecting merchant ship. 'Start the attack!'

'Fire one!' The boat shuddered. 'Torpedo running, sir!' Dreyfus called.

'Time?'

'Ten thirty, sir!'

At that precise moment, under Thomas Holbrook's direction, the *Lady Priscilla* altered forty degrees to starboard, commencing the first leg of her zig-zag pattern. The 21-inch torpedo, packed with 1600lbs of high explosive, ran harmlessly down the port side of the merchant ship, heading for the shores of Africa at 28 knots.

Captain James Walton bit through the stem of his pipe and reached for the alarm button as, white faced, he watched the deadly wake speed past his ship. Strident bells clamoured throughout the ship, bringing an immediate response of pounding feet as officers and crew rushed to their action stations. Barely three minutes elapsed before a breathless 2nd Officer came pounding up the bridge ladder to report, 'All guns closed up, sir!'

Having due regard to her largely peaceable role, the *Lady Priscilla*'s armament was impressive. Her main defence consisted of a 12-pounder gun mounted on the forecastle head and a long-barreled 4-inch at the stern. Two quick-firing, 20mm Oerlikons on the bridge and twin, water-cooled, .5

calibre Vickers machine guns on each side of the boat deck supplemented the heavier guns. On the face of it then, the *Lady Priscilla* was well able to defend herself against the attack from the air or sea. In reality, the guns, with the exception of the Oerlikons, were elderly leftovers from World War I, having very limited reliability and capability. But the real weakness lay in the men who manned these guns. They were merchant seamen, seagoing civilians caught up in a holocaust which was not of their making. A three-day course at the RN gunnery school at Chatham had taught them the rudiments of loading and laying their guns but, in no sense of the word, could they be deemed to be trained gunners.

U-316 lay stopped at 14 metres, her control room silent and brooding. Willy Mueller straightened up from the useless periscope, his face grey with disappointment. His only ace had been cruelly trumped. 'Stand by to surface,' he said quietly.

James Walton drew in a sharp, horrified breath as the rust-streaked conning tower broke the surface half a mile on the port beam. For fully five seconds, he watched spellbound, then he erupted into action. 'Hard-a-starboard!' he roared. 'Open fire with the 4-inch.!'

Under the circumstances, Walton was adopting the only course open to him, short of surrendering. He had decided to put his stern on to the enemy and fight a running battle. But his courageous action was doomed from the start. The barrel of the *Lady Priscilla*'s 4-inch exploded with the first round, killing the entire gun's crew. In the excitement of the stand-to, the untrained gunners had omitted to remove the watertight tampon from the muzzle of the gun.

The casing was still awash as *U-316*'s gun crew splashed forward to man the 105mm deck gun. Mueller grabbed his 1st lieutenant's arm as he left the conning tower to take charge on deck. 'Six rounds, Horst! Remember that! Make every one count!'

The U-boat's diesels coughed into life, drawing air in through the conning tower hatch with a rush. Mueller bent to the voicepipe. 'Port ten! Full ahead together! Steady!' The submarine surged forward, rapidly picking up speed to her maximum of 18 knots. The chase was on.

Walton tore his eyes away from the carnage of the poop deck, blind rage sweeping over him. Those men had been *his* men—his children. Every one had been with him through six long, weary years of war, willingly sharing the hardships, the dangers, the brain-numbing fatigue. Now they were no more than fragments of bloody flesh and splintered bone. He turned to watch the U-boat, fast gaining on him, and shook his fist. 'I'll fight you, you heathen, murdering bastard!' he roared. There was no thought of surrender in his head. He swung on his heel. 'Mister Holbrook!'

Holbrook, his face lined with strain, appeared at the captain's elbow. 'Yes, sir?'

'Get for'ard to the 12-pounder and see if you can get those buggers to shoot straight. I'm going to get this bastard if it's the last thing I do. Load and fire as fast as you can. Right?'

Holbrook nodded and tightened the chinstrap of his steel helmet.

'And, Tom . . .,' Walton's voice softened.

'Yes, sir?'

'Good luck!'

The first shell from *U-316*'s gun flew over the *Lady Priscilla* at mast-top height, as she turned to bring her own gun to bear. 'Down 300!' Mueller roared.

The 12-pounder fired with a whip-like crack, sending its puny missile spinning over the U-boat to explode in a flurry of water 250 yards on the far side of the submarine. 'You're too bloody high!' Walton shouted from the bridge.

The two opposing guns fired in unison. Both shells fell short.

U-316 was quickly pulling up on the weaving merchant ship. Mueller pounded the leaping edge of the conning tower with his fist. 'Why doesn't the stupid bastard surrender?' he growled through clenched teeth. 'Up 100! Fire!'

The German shell landed close alongside the *Lady Priscilla*, throwing spray high over her bridge. Walton ducked, his bowels constricting as he thought of the explosives contained within the thin, steel sides of his holds. He raised his head, wiping salt spray from his eyes. The U-boat appeared to be drawing off, perhaps deterred by the peppering she was receiving from the *Lady Priscilla*'s peashooter, which seemed to have found the range at last.

But Willy Mueller was far from deterred. He was merely manouvering into position for the kill. His gun too had found the range. Now, with only three shells remaining, Mueller was poised to use all his skill and experience. The merchant ship turned slowly to port, presenting her full silhouette. Mueller cupped his hands around his mouth. 'Fire!'

The shell passed through the *Lady Priscilla*'s funnel without exploding, but further weakening the storm-damaged structure. Walton glanced anxiously up at the tall, grey painted smokestack. Above the frenzied thump of the engines, he could hear ominous creaking sounds. Was it his imagination, or was the whole thing swaying with each heel of the ship? The arrival of *U-316*'s penultimate shell tore his mind away from the problem. The missile exploded in the wheelhouse, filling the place with smoke and flame and turning the helmsman and the officer of the watch into an intermingled mess of bloody flesh. Deafened by the blast, Walton was thrown bodily against the brass pedestal of the engineroom telegraph and slid to the deck barely conscious. Drunkenly, he clawed his way upright. He became aware of a frightening numbness in his left arm. He looked down. Below the elbow there was nothing. From the shredded stump of his upper arm great gouts of blood oozed out to fall lazily to the deck, staining the scrubbed teakwood bright red.

Walton's stunned mind struggled to assess the situation. He was terribly wounded, many of his men were gone, his ship was being slowly pounded to pieces and unable to defend herself. To save the ship and those still alive, he must surrender. He must heave to and surrender. His remaining hand grasped the telegraph handle and pulled. The handle did not move. It was jammed fast in the full ahead position.

Willy Mueller allowed himself a grim smile. He had her now. The hit on her bridge had either killed the occupants or knocked out the steering gear, for the merchant ship was now turning in a lazy circle. The next shell—his last—must strike squarely below the waterline and preferably in her engineroom. This was his final chance to land the sitting duck. Handing over the con to his junior lieutenant, Mueller jumped to the casing and ran forward.

'All right, Horst . . . I'll take it!' he shouted, pushing the startled Dreyfus to one side. He bent over the telescopic sight, laying the gun with trembling hands but with neat precision. His target was the waterline of the merchant vessel, directly below her tall funnel. Behind those plates lay the most vulnerable section of the ship's hull; the cavernous engine spaces which, once breached, would flood at an unstoppable pace. Mueller squeezed the trigger.

In his last pain-wracked, conscious moments, Captain James Walton had dragged himself to the engineroom voice-pipe and given the order to stop engines. The way fell off the ship at once and Mueller's carefully aimed shell—the final round—missed its intended target and ploughed deep into Number Three hatch, immediately forward of the bridge. In that hatch, laid side by side on top of the bags of cement, were eight hundred 250lb bombs.

The *Lady Priscilla* blew apart with a thunderous roar. Her great funnel, weakened by storm and shell, sheered off at its base and went spinning 500 feet into the air.

The cheers of Kapitan-Leutnant Mueller and his crew turned to shrieks of horror as the smoke-blackened, steel cylinder reached the apex of its trajectory and turned slowly over to begin its descent. Plummeting down from the sky like some giant, malevolent harpoon, the fifty tons of curved steel struck *U-316* amidships, crushing her fragile hull and forcing it down, down into the bottomless depths of the Indian Ocean.

Four thousand miles away, on a morning vibrant with the approach of summer, the joyful bells of victory rang out across the island kingdom of Britain. It was the 8th day of May, 1945.